AN AUTUMN AT LAKE ANN

By Dan Bales

ISBN 1-58961-015-6

Avaliable at your favorite bookstore or contact:
Published by PageFree Publishing, Inc.
733 Howard Street
Otsego, Michigan 49078
616-692-3386
www.pagefreepublishing.com

Dec. 2002

For Sandy and Jon

I am humbled and honored
each time someone asks to
purchase this little book.
Your generosity with your money and
time are deeply appreciated.

Cordially,
Dan

ACKNOWLEDGEMENTS

This is my first book. I am indebted to many people because I had so much to learn:

Ross and Jeannette Albert; John Pettit; Stoney and Sherill Thornburg; Mike Sorrell; Judy Patterson; and my nephew, Travis Ernest, all contributed information, time and talent that I did not have. Mitch Anderson and Kent Robinson have long thought I was capable of writing a book. Freelance editor, Nicole Rodino was helpful beyond description.

Elkhart author Tim Miller suggested I contact Kim Blagg at Page Free Publishing, Inc. A fortunate choice indeed. She and her associate, Jon Paul Jones, have been exceedingly kind and helpful to this first time author.

My brother Chris took my photo for the back cover.

The awesome front cover is the handiwork of local artist Rosanna McFadden.

Karl Marsh, Mark and Becky Troyer, Wade and

Marilyn Geyer, Phyllis Mooreland, and Susan Moriarty, all read or graciously listened, as I read this book to them. To my dad, his wife, and my siblings for the life's experiences that provided starting points in creating this story.

Mostly, I'd like to thank Becky, my wife. I met her when we were kids. She is the center point of my universe. All of my experiences, explorations, and achievements have relevance only because I can return to her love to understand their influence on my life.

It is only fitting then, as I finish this book, just before our 25th wedding anniversary; I dedicate it to her. Becky, this is for you.

Happy Anniversary!

CHAPTER 1
A PONTOON BOAT, AND A CAR

Hazel had sat down beside me, taking a break from cleaning dishes. She slung her dishtowel over her shoulder, put her arm around me, and we chatted a bit. Soon we had run out of things to say, and sat together in a comfortable silence. As she reached for her dishtowel and began to move, I was jolted from that pleasant moment and realized that it could have been one second or a couple of minutes. Although I was staring blankly ahead, I was looking toward Rich Franken, and he was looking uneasily at me.

The church basement was set with rows of tables and folding chairs. Dozens of folks had eaten, visited, and then left. Rich was the only one eating. He had just started. In our community, after graveside services, we usually had a big meal in the church basement. Rich never got to see the whole feast spread, he came late. He was the gravedigger. He had just finished covering up Mom's grave. I got up and walked to the coffeepot for a refill, then went and sat with Rich.

"Sorry Rich, I hadn't meant to stare in your direction I was just in my own world I guess."

"I figured," said Rich, "but then, I wasn't sure and was hoping I hadn't dumped baked beans on my shirt or something." He smiled.

"At the end of a funeral day, you just run out of words," Rich said, looking down at his plate.

We sat silently for awhile then I glanced at him and realized we were both watching Hazel drying dishes.

A man of simple truth, Rich leaned toward me and said, "Kinda looks like a big cat latched onto her arms, and she's tryin' to shake 'em off."

Embarrassed, but amused, I shook my head then laughed.

At her usual intuitive best, Hazel, looking our way, had thrown the dishtowel over her shoulder, put her hands on her waist, and snapped her huge hips left to right in a parodied seductiveness that had made us all laugh.

Hazel had these huge arms. Dangling below her triceps was this big jiggly, well, blubber. It sort of danced as she wiped the dishes or briskly stirred a pot; mesmerizing really.

This giant of a woman was equally equipped with compassion. She never had any children yet I thought the whole town felt somehow mothered by her.

Hazel was Mom's best friend. She had been widowed in her first few years of marriage. Her husband, Ernie Mowry, had been in a fatal traffic accident. He played the clarinet in a swing band that traveled throughout the Midwest. Usually she went with him on his tours, and often sang with the band, but wasn't along when Ernie was killed. Hazel never remarried. She had told Mom, that Lake Ann was like a paradise, but lacked refined and cultured black men. She belonged to a generation that was cautious with the bi-racial dating and marriage issue. As an older woman she found the times had changed, as well as her own attitudes.

Yet, in current days, she responded to anyone suggesting a possible suitor; "Now what on earth do I want with some wrinkled up old man, black, or white?"

Hazel was a warm and fun-loving person. She sang, played the piano, organ, and violin. She stopped tap dancing some hundred pounds and a few years ago.

When tragedy would strike someone, she would be there with food. In the past she headed up the summer flotilla festival and along with Mom, the Lake Ann Community Organic Gardening Club. She had a way of mobilizing people. As Mom's best friend, my sister and I were naturally on the receiving end of her great kindness and her genuine interest in our lives.

In fact many years ago, Dad, Mom, Liz and I all stayed with Hazel for a few days one winter. Our garage had a register in the wall near the top of the steps leading into the house. It was always falling off, and on one such occasion our black cat, Fluffy, decided to investigate the source of the pleasant warmth that flowed from that hole. Poor Fluffy slid helplessly down the furnace duct and collided with the spinning furnace fan. None of us ever heard a noise.

In those days, Liz used to wash her hair in the morning and then stand over a register waiting for the furnace to run. She would rub her hair briskly in the warm air coming out of the register. It gave her that great "poofy" look that teens in the late 60's and early 70's found so fashionable. I walked past her and noticed hair flying everywhere. "Lizzie your hair's falling out!" Like most teen-age girls with younger brothers she responded with a sneer and a command: "Shut up turd brain!"

By the time Liz and I had gotten off of the school bus that afternoon, Mom was in the car, parked in the driveway, waiting for us. We approached the car in silence and gawked at our house. It was in the dead of winter and all of the windows in the house were wide open. Drapes fluttered in the wind.

Earlier that day the repairman had tried to clean Fluffy's remains from the furnace, but kept getting sick from the stench. Finally he opened all of the windows, turned the furnace up all the way and promised to return the next day.

We ended up staying with Hazel for three or four days.

Fluffy was the last cat to ever live in Will and Grace Bahle's home.

All at once my mind was full of thoughts. I was happy Hazel lived in my town. I doubted people ever outgrew the need for another person who represented a mother image. Flooded again with emotion, I had sensed a hollow in the pit of my stomach. I sure missed my mom.

"Some graves are hard to open - like for a child - shouldn't be doin' it, ya know. Some are hard to close, like ya can't really get sorted out that it's the last goodbye. Your mom you know," said Rich, "was about the hardest grave to open and to close."

Rich had gone to high school with my mom, although he was younger. Mom had told us that Rich had wanted to date her back in those days, but she kept a casual attitude towards him. It was evident to my sister and me, however, ever since we were old enough to understand such matters, that Rich silently adored Mom. We watched him when he came to

Mom and Dad's store, how he would never take his eyes off Mom as she waited on him at the deli or from behind the meat counter. He lived alone and quietly and few people had the chance to notice the depth of his kindness.

I remember once, he was mowing grass at the cemetery with a push mower. As I drove past while on a visit home from college, I stopped to inquire why he wasn't using "Old John". "Old John" was his pride and joy. A John Deere riding mower with chrome hubcaps, a chrome brush guard grill, chromed diamond plate front fenders, a radio, and one of those knobs on the steering wheel. It always shined of recent waxing.

"Sold it," said Rich. Probably I had continued to prod and push for details a bit too much; Rich broke down and wept that his only sister had a daughter who had recently died of cancer. Expenses were burdensome and there wasn't any life insurance.

"No family of mine's gonna have to forego a proper burial," said Rich. He had sold his treasured tractor, which he also used in his duties as Sexton of the township's cemetery, to provide money for his niece's funeral over a thousand miles away.

Later that day I remember telling my sister, mom, and dad of this simple, silent act of grace by a simple, silent man. In no time Mom was on the phone with Hazel, and while I never knew all of the details, I'm fairly sure some of the bluebloods were brow beat into participation in a scheme concocted by Mom and Hazel for Rich's benefit.

I understand it was only days later Rich had a new John Deere provided by the township for maintaining the cemetery. And another one given to him personally which he kept at home. Very soon both had become customized with the glitzy chrome and personal touches of Rich Franken.

While it is customarily considered bad manners to leave your "free" hand on the table while you eat, I was glad Rich had such a posture. I reached for his meaty hand and squeezed. He looked up from the plate and tears welled up in his eyes.

"Thanks Rich," I spoke softly. Not by intent, but that's all that would come out. I stood and walked over to Hazel who embraced me with one of her life affirming hugs. When I was young I viewed her hugs as life threatening. Breathing would cease not only because you were powerless to expand your diaphragm, but because your face was buried deeply in her ample bosom. Meanwhile your dangling feet slung about like a rag doll until she planted you back down on them. In a moment you would breathe again, feel your legs, and move to a more secure location. Now, grown up, I yearned for a hug like Hazel's. To be enveloped for an instant by this combination of flesh and compassion was to know for that instant peace, security, and acceptance. All encompassing love you could say, both literally and figuratively.

Dad and Liz, my sister, had left the funeral dinner well ahead of me. As I headed for Dad's place to meet them, I drove past Bahle's Meat and Deli. A closed sign was on the front door; another tiny symbol that produced such a big shockwave along my spine. Mom was gone.

I got out of the car at Dad's and walked around to the front of the house. I knew Dad and Liz would be on the deck along the lake. I heard a loud crack, the unmistakable sound of a gunshot. My pace quickened. Liz was sitting on a lawn chair with her 20-gauge shotgun on her shoulder. As I got closer I yelled "Liz, what the hell is going on?"

"The hell is I'm out of scotch and Dad went in to pour me some!"

"Shotgun," I said.

"Oh," she began, "Mom wanted some of those lower limbs trimmed out of the old cottonwood. Kinda been hanging low, blocks the view from the picture window."

She turned and spat. I laughed as she turned back around. She had been chewing on a big, fat, cut-off cigar. Aside from her shotgun and scotch, as she spat her hand bent upward slightly at the wrist, was the unmistakable gesture indicative of the femininity and grace exuding from the complex and comic character before me.

Liz had always lived at home, except for her college years. She worked part time as a registered nurse at the community hospital, part time as a veterinarian assistant at the animal clinic our granddad Dotson had started a generation ago. Liz actually was a veterinarian, and even worked with Granddad before he had quit practicing. One time, when patching up Bert Smith's old Shepherd "Mike," Liz had to practically reconstruct an ear. Mike used to like to find coyotes and give them as Bert said, "A what-to-for," then make his wounded way home. Anyway, Liz repaired the ear of old Mike. Shortly thereafter, Bert's grandkids were over. One of his granddaughters, who was quite young, reached over and petted old Mike's head. He turned on her. Aside from the pain of the wound and the stitches, what bothered Liz, as she visited the little girl in the hospital, was the trauma and confusion of Mike's betrayal. Liz became a registered nurse and earned a master's degree in counseling psychology, but not before she and Granddad paid a visit to Bert to talk about old Mike. Bert loved his old Shepherd but felt that when one family member betrayed the others then that family member needed to be dealt with.

"He's got to go," Bert told Granddad.

So Liz and Granddad took old Mike to the clinic. Old Mike got his burrs all brushed out and he chewed on a bone, his last day.

Dad, having seen me while inside the house brought an unmarked brown bottle in one hand and Liz's scotch in the other.

"Dopple Bock," he spoke as he handed me the bottle. Dad brewed beer periodically and it was always a pleasure to have one in his company. He judged his quality by your facial expressions, and how you swallowed. He beamed when you seemed to savor his home brewed creations.

"Lizzie's getting to the trimming," he said pointing up. "Twenty gauge slugs kinda tears the hell out of the limbs, but it opens the view all the way to heaven."

Hearing what he had just said, and feeling the weight of it, he dropped his arm suddenly. We all sat silent for a long, long, time.

Liz broke the silence, "Granddad told me Mom could shoot, you know, when he was teaching me."

"I probably spoiled that," Dad smiled, "somehow your granddad thought that since I was a meat cutter I would be a hunter and a fisherman too. So he wanted to take me rabbit hunting. It was late fall and there was a little dust of snow. He handed me a shotgun as we got out of the car. We took a couple of steps and he knelt down."

"Will, see these tracks? At the other end of 'em is your dinner!" He grinned and stood up.

"Well we were off to the chase, I was a rabbit hunter. All of a sudden I stopped."

"I don't even know how to shoot this thing!" I said.

"He looked at me like I was green and had one eye in the middle of my head. Then he grinned that grin of his and told me to lean up against this one tree, I did. Then he said to hold the gun up, but keep it a foot or so from your shoulder. I did that too. Then he showed me the safety, stepped back, and told me to squeeze off a shot. As I fell down to my knees with pain I saw him laugh so hard he actually pissed himself. You always hold the gun butt to your shoulder, hold it away and the recoil kicks like a mule. That was the end of hunting and shooting for me. As I far as I know, Hazel was the only person he ever told what a shooter I was. They happened to be in the store at the same time and he told Hazel to ask me about my rabbit hunting. I told your granddad I would, but first he should tell his great pants pissing story! Hazel suggested we work on it together and let her know when we wanted to tell her the whole story. That never happened."

Granddad Dotson was a character. He was a wise-ass. Liz certainly was his granddaughter. He was also very bright, and an original thinker.

As a veterinarian, granddad watched agricultural practices change. Animal husbandry was, of course, his greatest concern. He was alarmed that feeds became routinely supplemented with hormone like substances, and antibiotics. He believed that some-day public health would be affected. Feedlot run-offs would enter waterways from where cities and towns obtained drinking water. He wondered what might happen if low levels of antibiotics came into contact with bacteria, and without killing them, caused them to mutate into drug resistant and viru-lent strains. He contemplated epidemics. He urged Mom and Dad to work hard to find sources of healthy, pasture fed beef, pork, and chicken. As best as they were able, they took his advice. Mom and Dad were always proud to sell meat to their custom-ers that hadn't been raised on factory farms.

In terms of enterprise, Dad came to realize an-other benefit as well. Though pasture fed beef, and especially organic grown made his prices higher than the chain stores. It helped control the business vol-ume so that he and Mom could handle the workload without an extra crew of meat cutters and wrappers. He held onto an acceptable profit margin, and held his cost of labor in check.

Mom continued granddad's passion and concern for safe and pure food. She and Hazel had founded the Lake Ann Community Organic Gardening Club. We got to eat anything left after the rabbits, squir-rels, and raccoons ate their fill. Mom's broccoli was once attacked by little green worms we called "cab-bage loopers." She or Hazel had read somewhere that you could mash a bug and its digestive system would rupture of course, but in the digestive tract might be bacteria unfriendly to the bug itself. Their theory was to mash a bunch of the bugs, strain the liquid and spray it on the broccoli, thereby creating their own epidemic. Armed with a blender, a strainer, and a spray bottle Mom and Hazel went about their gardening making a veritable health hell for the insect world. Liz's favorite joke at that time was: "Know what's green and goes six hundred miles an hour? cabbage loopers in a blender."

"Max, I want you to think about the store again."

I was stunned. Liz didn't look at me, just wiggled back into her chair, amused with the prospect of how I would respond. The folks periodically tried to convince me to come home to Lake Ann and join them in the store. It was a matter of pride to Dad; he had bought it from his dad.

At least there would never be a bid to Liz, and the resulting sibling problem. Liz was good in crisis. But waiting and watching a customer choose pork chops from the meat case and anguish over it didn't merit "crisis" as far as Liz was concerned. As the folks used to tell the story over, and over through the years: Apparently in high school Liz worked behind the counter and impatiently waited on Mrs. Monroe. Untying her apron and throwing it down she yelled, "For the sake of the sanity of the free world Mrs. Monroe, make up your mind! Bake a damned ham!" And she stormed out of the store. The folks thought it was best she not attend the counter after that.

I, on the other hand, got along just fine with the customers.

Lake Ann was a resort community. Located in northern Indiana, it was the infamous hideout for Al Capone during the prohibition era years when Chicago's gang scene had become competitive and murderous. There was of course gambling, abundant liquor, great food and the finest in dance hall entertainment. While many lake resorts of the time throughout the mid-west held family themed spiritual renewals or Chautauqua's Lake Ann was loud and rowdy and yet expansive enough that no one seemed especially troubled when big city underworld types showed up in the summer. It was during those years that Grandpa Bahle started selling dressed chickens, smoked meats, sausages, and hot dogs to summer cottage residents. First out of a wagon he brought to town, then from the front porch of some family's home, which he eventually bought and turned into a meat store and deli. When my dad was young, the store burnt down and a modest brick building was constructed in its place. Eventually, this became the main business district, even though it had grown to only about two blocks long. Gift shops, coffee shops, a pharmacy, two banks, a hardware store, three nice restaurants, and of course, a bait and tackle shop completed the mix. At the edge of town you would find the chain store pharmacy, convenience store, gas station, veterinarian, town hall, attorney, elementary and high school and the small hospital. A few miles south was Elkton, the county seat, a larger community with great distinction. The Sears and Roebuck as well as Montgomery Ward catalog were formerly printed there. More eggs were produced and shipped from the surrounding area than from anywhere else in the nation. Eventually, it became famous for its industries producing most of the world's artificial replacement hips and knees. This was the world from which I came, the world that my parents and older sister loved. The world they continuously beckoned my return to.

As I said, I was attending my mother's funeral. Her death was a sudden, shocking incident. She had drowned.

After Labor Day when the summer residents would have nearly all returned to their permanent homes, the Lake Ann community had a different pace of life. While commerce and area merchants realized the importance of the affluent summer tourist trade, it was frenetic and there was a kind of community sigh as the traffic thinned out, the lake grew still of boating activity, and the town's stores and shops became places where local people visited with each other.

As the days grew short and the nights chilly the water temperature fell quickly. Only the most robust would swim or water ski. But on those wonderful days when the sun shone bright and the wind was still, a slow ride on the pontoon boat was one of Mom's greatest pleasures. The day she died was such a day.

Mom had announced to Dad at the store that it "… surely was too nice of an afternoon for work," and had packed a fabulous lunch from the deli. She had called Liz, and Emma Walker; her dear childhood friend, to meet her at home, "For a cruise." It was something the three of them had done often over the years. It truly was the kind of thing that a person should do, if at all possible. Floating on a sunlit lake that glistened as though with shoebox sized diamonds scattered about, and viewing the wooded areas of the shoreline with the trees beginning to shift color from all greens to yellows, oranges and reds.

A ride around the lake had some kind of restorative power for the human spirit. It was for many folks, including Liz, Emma, and my mom, a sort of spiritually enriching experience each time.

As was their routine, they navigated the pontoon boat to whatever location of the lake suited them. Mom usually piloted her and dad's pontoon.

She would kill the engine then move to the front of the boat and pitch an anchor in. The last time she threw an anchor, however, something in the water distracted her. The boat shadowed the water next to it, and she thought she saw a flash; something shiny, just before the anchor splashed through the surface.

"How odd…" Mom spoke to Liz and Emma as she stepped across the deck rail and stood on the front of the pontoon tube looking down into the water.

Liz and Emma glanced to the road, off the other side of the boat in the direction of a car's horn. They waved, although not sure at whom. The car advanced around the curve up the incline over the bridge where Indian Creek entered the lake. As they turned around, the boat rocked and Mom disappeared into the lake. Liz and Emma leapt up, Emma could spring into action as quickly as any person could, but would immediately begin some roll of banter. "Oh this isn't good Liz. It is not good. Oh dear god, oh Liz this is not good." She spoke as she pulled the flotation seat cushion off to use it to throw to Mom.

"We're just going to fish her out; no sweat." Liz said as they moved from the back up to the front of the boat.

"Oh my god!" Liz quickly pulled off her sweatshirt, kicked off her deck shoes, and dove into the blood stained water. Mom had lost her footing and slipped off the pontoon. Probably she tried to catch herself and arched backwards. Her head hit the mooring yoke welded on the pontoon near the front. Unconscious, she slipped through the fifteen feet or so of grassy water landing on the hood of a car.

"Emma! Help me!" Liz shouted and gasped for air as she resurfaced and broke through the water. The two of them managed to get Mom onto the boat deck. As Liz tried to resuscitate Mom, Emma stood at the controls, unaware that she was still clutching anchor rope after hurriedly bringing it up. Liz quickly moved towards her purse and grabbed her cell phone and started to dial.

"Let's get to the landing Em'," Liz said as she dialed. Stamping her feet in frustration, Emma pushed the throttle as if exertion could yield more speed. Tears flowed down her face. The sound coming from her lips and mouth that wouldn't move was soft, but meaningful, if only to her. "Oh God, oh God." Emma seemed to groan.

"Emergency dispatch? This is Liz Bahle, get an EMS unit to the north shore landing. Do it! Now! While I hold! Okay. Can you patch me through to the crew? Then put the damned earpiece you're wearing next to the radio. Just do it! Hello! This is Liz Bahle, I'm on a boat heading to north shore landing. My mom is unconscious and bleeding from her head.

You better be ready! That stretcher better be at the waters edge with an oxygen tank on it or I'll pin your EMS badges to your ..." An exasperated Liz stopped short from saying God only knows what. She continued to work on Mom. She dialed the phone again and handed it to Emma.

"Ask for Dad Em', tell him to get to north shore."

"Will! Will! It's Emma. Come to north shore landing. It's not good Will!"

The two EMS responders were standing in the water holding the gurney, looking alternately at each other and at the fast approaching pontoon. They listened as the motor, at full throttle, didn't seem to be slowing. They began to move out of the water, slowly, then quickly, as the pontoon suddenly screeched partway up the cement incline. The men jumped onto the deck and knelt beside a sobbing Liz.

"She's gone." Frozen, the two men waited for Liz to bark out some orders. She didn't. Instead they stood and took a shaking, almost convulsing Emma from the boat.

Liz pretty much had the local EMS and emergency personnel on alert. She knew her work well. She thought ahead and had no tolerance for wasted motion or lack of preparedness in emergency response work. Many of the volunteer EMS people had been reprimanded by her at one time or another whether it was while she was on duty at the hospital, or if a close friend of hers was treated less than flawlessly and she later heard about it. Liz had no problem bluntly enlightening people when she rationalized it was in the best interest of "the person, or the world they live in, which includes me."

By this time the police chief had shown up; and Dad. Dad went directly to the boat where Liz awaited him; alongside Mom. The chief gave them the courtesy of a few private moments and spoke with the EMS crew and Emma. The chief escorted a blanket wrapped Emma to his car then radioed the dispatcher.

"We're gonna need to get a dive team here tomorrow first thing. Better call the coroner, and try to line up a tow service. We need a wrecker with a lot of cable. Appears we've got a car in the weeds on the bottom of Lake Ann."

Dad and Liz rode in the ambulance to the hospital, where Mom was pronounced dead. The chief made arrangements for someone to get the boat out of launch and have it moored at its dock at Mom and Dad's home. Then he took Emma home. Emma called Hazel who called Rich; Hazel also called Pastor Brock, who called the priest, Old Father Joe. And by morning, long before folks bothered to read the newspaper or turn on the radio, most people around town knew of my mother's death, and the mysterious car, in the weeds at the bottom of Lake Ann.

The police chief, Ted Armstrong, was one of Dad's cronies. Neither Ted nor Dad were members of lodges or service clubs. They were fierce individualists. Dad always seemed to know when a family had money problems, and quietly he assisted families over the years with food from his store.

Chief Armstrong used similar discretion and compassion in carrying out his duties. One night he stopped the operator of a local marina for drunk driving. The man was having a well-publicized spat with his hot-tempered wife that summer. He had gotten very intoxicated, had thrown up on himself and soiled himself as well. Fearing his wife's wrath if he went home in such a condition, he decided to drive around town and shortly thereafter was stopped by Chief Armstrong. The chief suggested it was a fine evening for a walk, and grabbing a blanket from his squad car, walked with the man to the lake. The man was told to take off his shoes and take everything out of his pockets and put in them. Next, the chief told him to go into the water up to his butt and get undressed, then throw his clothes as far as he could. He was told to wash himself up then come onto shore and wrap up in the blanket. As the men walked back to the squad car, the chief told the man he needed a bath more than he needed to be arrested. The chief took him home and announced to the man's wife that it appeared that her husband had gone for a swim, and someone took his clothes. He instructed the wife to put on some coffee and see if she and her husband could figure out how they had come to this point in their day.

Dad was with Liz at home when she phoned me. at work. I worked at Acme-Archer, a manufacturer of rubber gaskets for oil filters where I scheduled the production for the factory. Acme-Archer was the oldest factory and largest manufacturing employer in Greenfield, the city where I also lived, about two hours away.

I recall having telephoned the company president at the local country club. While I had his cell phone number, I called instead the number of the lounge at the country club. He was there having cocktails. I had suspected that his time spent in the lounge zenithed his time on the links.

"You're on your own a few days old man," I told him. "I have to go back home. My mom passed." I began to choke.

"Get home Maxie boy, we'll take care of things. Hey, what can we do for you? Anything! Just say the word!" the old man said.

Heartbroken and also pissed off, I recall thinking that what he could do is hire an assistant so that the department foremen could know what to do when I wasn't there. I had been the assistant until my predecessor retired a few years back. When I assumed the position of production scheduler, an assistant was never hired. I was rarely ill, and had accumulated over 480 unused vacation hours. This was one of those defining moments in life, when nothing is more important than being home. I couldn't recall the words Liz and I exchanged on the phone. Couldn't recall racing back to my apartment to pack then driving to Lake Ann. But I would always recall the thought that swept over me as I walked through the door to the folks house; Mom would never be there; or at the store, ever again.

Dad, Liz, and I alternately wept and warmed the coldness of our grief with the knowledge that Mom died in a place she loved, on a picture perfect day. She and two people who mutually cared for and enjoyed one another's company. Later on we called the funeral director and took care of arrangements. Eventually that night we all went to bed and slept the restless sleep shared by the grieving, the forlorn, and the troubled. We would rise to a new morning, but days and nights and the value of time were rendered temporarily meaningless by the seemingly surreal experience we were enmeshed within. Time seemingly stood still until the affiliated tasks were completed.

But the next day, the car in Lake Ann was too much of a curiosity in our little town, even in our personal grief, for Dad, Liz, and me to simply ignore.

I remember waking up to clattering from the kitchen. Liz and I emerged about the same time from our rooms and found Dad in the kitchen putting on coffee. He looked at us blankly and said, "I don't know what to do about Margo. She went back to Indianapolis to move more things here to the house that she recently bought. I don't even know her last name." Dad truly cared that Margo needed to be informed of Mom's death, but it was also brutally apparent to him that this was one of those things that Mom just did. She had hired Margo just weeks earlier, and of course, was to train her. Margo had closed the deal on a very nice lake house and was in the store where she struck up a conversation with Mom. Margo told of the real estate closing and her immediate move from Indianapolis to the lake. Mom had made them both coffee, and walked from behind the counter towards two chairs at a small table. She looked kindly and curiously at Margo, and spoke as an old friend. Beckoning for further details, Mom said: "now there's more to it than that, honey."

Liz had met Margo, I hadn't.

"Dad," Liz began, "I'll go into the store and see what I can find. We'll get in touch with her," Liz assured him.

Meanwhile, we received many kind phone calls. A few folks dropped by with food. After a while we were able to leave the house. We stopped at the funeral home to receive assurance that all of the details were in order. Next, we were off to the store to tend with a few matters.

Dad fashioned a crude sign, which he hung on the front door of the store. "Due to the death of Grace Bahle, the store will be closed for a few days." Dad instructed us to cancel certain deliveries to the store, call the hospital, churches, and any place that could use the perishable products and get to them quick. Liz and I had our assignments, Pastor Brock agreed to arrive quickly and let people in to pick up the meat and deli products, which Dad specified, needed to be eaten up before they "turned green".

Dad seemed very concerned about the store, and was quite emotionally charged. Mom had sometimes referred to the store as Dad's "first true love." But I was watching something else. Watching a man whose business partner, lover, and friend had just died. He was immersing himself into the familiar work setting he shared with Mom. He sought every remnant of her former presence there. It seemed that he had an anxiousness mixed with confusion, and wished that Mom would walk through the door returning his blissful life to him. He wept. So did Liz and I.

Dad recounted many things about he and Mom's store as Liz and I intently listened. He told us about ways in which the business changed over the years. He described how Grandma used to can meat because many customers liked to use canned meat in stews, soup, or with noodles. Dad laughed when telling about Grandpa instructing the slaughterhouse to save the spleens from hogs. He would grind all of the pork fat with some lean meat for sausage, then, throw the spleen into the grinder mixing its bright colored liquid into the meat. It yielded a bright pink, delectable looking meat.

"Your Mom put her foot down when we took over the store. She said there wouldn't be any entrails in our bulk sausage. Pork is leaner nowadays than it was back then. People wouldn't put up with frying all that fat anymore," Dad said.

"Was that about the time you cut yourself, Dad?" Liz asked.

"Somewhere along there I guess," Dad began, "Your Mom and I hadn't been married too long I know. Funny thing, I never cut myself too bad cutting meat. I was actually chopping cabbage for your Grandma. She used to make sauerkraut here you know."

Neither Liz nor I remembered that. We only knew that Dad had a serious injury to his wrist. Once, when we were young, we were all in the yard playing baseball. Dad was showing off and flexing the bat. Suddenly he dropped it. Blood was running from his wrist. He wrapped it with his hankie as Mom ran to him. Liz and I were terrified.

Apparently, when the surgeon repaired the severed tendon with wraps of wire, following Dads' cabbage cutting mishap, there remained under his skin a sharp end on the surgical wire. With his best rendition of "the mighty Casey at bat," Dad's bat flexing was just the right motion for the sharp wire to actually cut him from the inside out. Dad told us that Granddad Dotson used to say that as a horse doctor he could've done a better job than the quack who patched him up.

We left the store and drove around the east side of Lake Ann to the road block and pulled off the road onto the shoulder as dozens of other cars had.

When Mom had slipped off the pontoon as she peered down into the water that fateful day, she caught a glimpse of a car several feet down. We all were thinking that we hoped the dive team and wrecker crew would succeed in raising the car, because Dad, Liz, and I wanted to see the object of Mom's last curiosity.

The police chief and coroner were talking as we neared, and noticing us, they quickly moved in our direction; probably to put a bit of distance between themselves and the painstakingly slow operation and its beehive of interest and activity. Media and photo people spoke with local bystanders, sat on the hoods of cars, and generally enjoyed another warm, sunny, late summer's day.

The coroner's cell phone rang.

"Hello Father Joe, thanks for getting right back to me. You might want to get out here to the east side of the lake I think we've got one of yours in this car we're bringing up out of Lake Ann."

The coroner explained to us that most of the glass in the car was intact, including the windshield. The rear view mirror was still affixed and it had a rosary around it. Liz and the coroner began to "talk shop." The coroner said that divers noted heavy clothing including a winter coat slumped in the driver's seat. The weight of heavy, wet, fabric pushed on the body structure, and learning much more than I wanted to know, was told that as the body decomposes, bone separates from its jointed unions. Without tissue structure to maintain its skeletal form it just falls apart. This combined with the known presence of turtles, and divers having seen some "damned good size crayfish," suggested that natural decomposition was assisted by the animal kingdom.

I recall Liz asking the coroner about skulls sometimes not being found. I was astonished that she would have known anything about such matters. The coroner explained that when the skull separates from its adjoining structure, it might roll away, or float away by wave or water current action due to its relative size and shape as a spherical object.

Dad wandered off and was mingling with

townsfolk who were embracing him and treating him with the compassion he deserved that day. Wondering how to distance myself from Liz and the coroner's macabre conversation, I ended up being drawn to them as the tenor of the subject began to shift.

"The heater control was on the hot setting, on defrost, the fan on high." The coroner told Liz.

"Went in during winter," Liz suggested.

The coroner continued, "Boys from the dive team estimate by the condition of the car you know, rust, moss, and algae growth, that it has been in the water for maybe two or three years, maybe slightly more."

The dive team had taken underwater photos, and removed the remains as well as a steel box close to the victim's coat. The police chief, who had left Liz and the coroner, now returned to them.

"I've got your bag of bones, oh, sorry Liz. Father Joe is here. The boys are looking at a wallet. It had some laminated ID and we got a metal box with documents inside."

"Chief! Chief!" someone yelled. Then everyone started yelling for the chief at the same instant. The coroner and the police chief ran towards the commotion, Liz raced closed behind them. I was never the type to chase the fire truck; I walked towards Dad instead.

As the trio neared, Father Joe was sitting up.

"What the hell is going on!" The chief exclaimed.

One of the divers said, "The Father here asked if anyone knew the deceased's name. The boys found it on several things so I told him. Erik Von Rath we believe. He just closed his eyes and said 'blessed Mary and Joseph' and went out cold. He fainted."

Old Father Joe came around quickly. He made the sign of the cross and he spoke a tearful blessing and a prayer for the faithful departed. Father Joe turned to the coroner and asked, "Could you please take me home?" He reached toward her and the police chief. Looking at them both he said, "Then will you please both join me at the Clubhouse? I believe I have something for you." They agreed. The chief instructed a deputy to get the car up out of the lake and to get it to impound. "Tell the reporters we're wrapping it up here, we've got some evidence to sort out."

The coroner silently drove the priest to the rectory.

"I just don't feel like driving. Would you wait please, while I get something?"

"No problem," the coroner replied, "I'll be right here."

Soon the priest was back in the car and they drove off to the Clubhouse. The Clubhouse was a greasy, dark, smoky grill and tavern near the lake. It actually was called Billie's. It was a hangout for locals. It didn't appear to be very inviting and so the summer residents didn't "discover" it. Billie was the aging proprietor, bar keeper, grill cook, chain smoking, good-natured drunk who lived right next to it in a small cabin. She served an awesome breaded tenderloin sandwich. The meat was ordered twice a week from Dad's store, of course.

The old cronies such as my dad, Father Joe, and the police chief referred to Billie's as the "Clubhouse." I never asked whether they were mocking the country club set who summered on the lake, or if their title endeared their monthly card games. The group was fairly fluid but comprised mostly of the older merchants and political figures: Men.

My father invited the coroner, a young, middle aged single woman into the group. As the story lives on, he was feeling no pain while playing cards with some of the boys. In walked the coroner. It was very late at night after what was for her, a long, rough day. She bought a six pack to go. As she turned to leave and walked near them, one of the cronies spoke, (exactly which crony it was changes with the various versions of the story). He asked if she wanted to play some cards with them. The priest pointed out that it wasn't really the type of game for ladies. One of the cronies hollered: "hell, she's no lady, she's a politician."

The coroner slammed her beer onto the middle of their game, grabbed a chair from another table, sat down among them, bummed a cigarette from the priest, and broke out into laughter. She's been one of the cronies, one of the "old boys" ever since.

The coroner and Father Joe walked into the clubhouse and joined the police chief at a table.

"What'll it be boys?" Billie questioned.

"I suggest a bottle." said Father Joe.

"Scotch hon. The bottle. Three glasses. What's this about father?" the chief commanded.

The old priest closed his eyes and raised his hand, wanting to pause.

"Just a moment," the priest said.

Billie poured them each a shot, sat the bottle down, and dutifully returned to the bar and her burning cigarette. The priest drank deeply and poured himself another shot. He settled back into his chair and pulled a paper from his vest. He looked at the coroner and the chief.

"Do you remember after the blizzard four years ago, I asked you to inquire of other police agencies of accidents in the area? On the highways and the interstates?"

"You gotta be kidding me father!" The chief leaned on his elbows, which were placed on the table. Both hands clasped his glass.

The old priest's hands trembled as he straight-

ened out the letter. He took another drink then spread
the page out, smoothing it with his hands. His hands
came to rest on the margins and he leaned forward
and began to read.

Dear Father Joseph,
This will be my last letter to you.
In a few days I will say my goodbye
to Chicago and drive to Lake Ann.
Already I have practiced loading the car.
Everything fits in the back seat. I have
lived simply. As I said before, I
could have lived in an order of the church,
except for Mother and Father. I am 82
years old. What I have in this world
I will bring to Lake Ann. I will
bake bread at the retreat center
for my room. When my heavenly
father bids me come home, what
I have left, I will leave to your care.
I will attend Ash Wednesday mass here.
I will leave Chicago the next day.
Erik Von Rath

"Here's to Erik Von Rath," the coroner said. Two
others 'clinked' their glasses.

Four years ago last February the national
weather service recorded the lowest barometric pres-

sure in the history of the region. The wind howled and the snow fell in an unusually late winter snowstorm.

Not in the morning, but by afternoon there were whiteouts and even in the daytime you couldn't see a car length ahead. Then it cleared, but only for a few minutes until it was pure white again. This cycle continued past dark. No one was out and about, no one witnessed poor old Erik Von Rath drive deeper into the area's worst ever blizzard. No one saw his car slide out of control as he came over the Indian Creek Bridge, sliding over the thin ice that yielded to the water of Lake Ann. Within hours probably, the lake had enough ice to hold the snow that would conceal the reason why old Erik Von Rath never appeared at the Lake Ann Catholic Retreat Center. Until, that is, my mom discovered his car at the bottom of the lake.

Meanwhile, Dad, Liz and I had all gone back home. Liz suggested we call Margo. Liz had found her phone number when we had earlier been at the store.

"It's something I should do," Dad said, reaching for the piece of the paper that held Margo's phone number. "Stephens. Her name is Margo Stephens," Dad said as he dialed. After the third ring Margo answered. Dad then began the difficult task of telling her about Mom's death.

"I hardly know what to say Will," began Margo, "I've barely met you, but Grace and I talked about so many things and the way we felt about them. It seemed like I knew her longer. Will, if you need to change your mind about me"—

"Oh, Lord no Margo! How about just putting it off for a couple of weeks, how would that be?" Dad asked.

"Will, that would be fine, as long as you're sure. If you don't mind me saying Will, about this poor old man, maybe Grace would've wanted to be sure he didn't have to be buried without a ceremony, all alone."

"Margo, that's exactly how Grace would have thought. I am going to talk to the kids about this. Thanks Margo. See you in a couple of weeks. I'm going to need your help."

Describing this conversation with Margo, to Liz and me, Dad seemed confident that Mom's funeral should be a double billing with old Erik Von Rath. He talked about how Mom was a relationship and possibility kind of thinker who enjoyed connecting to other people and had a sincere sense of wonder and awe for those who had interesting passions they embraced quietly like Rich and his customized tractors. But she also encouraged those who were bolder like my sister Liz for example, who had a thirst for knowledge and understanding that led her into therapeutic conversation with pets, spirit liberation and affirmation therapies for people, regression therapy, and a wide variety of unconventional things. It was not surprising then that she was excited about this unusual funeral.

"Talk about corollaries, if you don't have any problems with this Max, I think we should meet Pastor Brock and old Father Joe and work this out." Liz was fully engaged.

The next day began visitation at the funeral home, first from 2-4 p.m., then from 6-8 p.m. Dad was having some problems, not the least of which was that he was unsure about how he could last through a workday without Mom, now that the summer help had left, mostly students, they had returned back to school.

Liz had suggested that people like Hazel could help at the deli or behind the meat case, that there would be a number of folks that might be able to help out part time.

"Maybe you could reduce the hours your store is open Dad," I suggested. Those words were thought up in the logic part of my brain then made their way to utterance. The words that followed seemed to come from somewhere else, as Dad, Liz and I all looked blankly at one another following my surprising statement.

"Maybe I could stay a couple of weeks and help,

Dad." Since getting the call from Liz telling me about Mom, perhaps my conscious rejection of being a butcher was being undermined by my subconscious desire to live among the people that I loved most, and who also cared for me. Those people whose lives had meaning in a personally gratifying sense, and in a sense of belonging to and being connected to one another, and to the lake. Few people would argue against the soothing nature of water. Whether immersed in it, floating on it, or allowing one's mind to become lost in its movement, all powerfully draw humankind and other creatures to it. Mankind as well as other mammals and many birds have since primitive times acknowledged bodies of water as sustainers and providers of life and nourishment. Perhaps this ancient comfort has been genetically encoded in us and we continue to be awed by water and to find ourselves easily reverent in its presence.

I was beginning to acknowledge that I had missed the lake. Even in the cold of winter it was a pleasure for the senses and spirit. The sun's rays glancing off the water multiplied the radiant nature of light and heat. It became like luminescent silver during a full moon.

Besides, I worked too much in Greenfield. When I went to work at Acme-Archer, I felt fortunate to move into an office job when I was dismissed from my teaching position. The events surrounding my firing were humiliating and defeating. So I had immersed myself in my production scheduling work. Before Acme-Archer, I had been teaching less then a year; high school Social Studies.

Early in the first semester I was calling a class to order. Suddenly, a male student leapt from his seat and attempted to restrain a girl directly across the aisle. He raised his fist and clenched a sharp pencil above her face. That was about the time I lunged on him. I struggled with him to the back of the room where he landed hard against the blackboard. The tray along the bottom of the chalkboard that holds the chalk and erasers broke, along with two of his ribs.

His parents said I was power abusive and explosive. The girl's parents said I lacked any understanding of classroom rules, and should have diffused the situation earlier, but as they accused, ignored it because she was black. The school system prevented a lawsuit by monitoring my classes weekly, putting me on probation for the rest of the year, and then firing me when school was out.

Four years of college, pre-in-the sky ideals, and my self worth dissolved into nothingness in an instant.

Alice, my fiancée, was a kindergarten teacher, also in the Greenfield school system. She and I grew up on Lake Ann, and were friends forever. In college we became lovers.

Greenfield hired both of us in the same week. It was an omen for us. We became engaged and decided we should save more money by sharing an apartment and we planned to marry at the end of our first year of teaching.

The probation and monitoring obviously made my first year emotionally draining. My lesson planning, grading criteria and discipline procedures had no room for flaws or errors. I didn't know I would be fired at the end of the year. The administration and teachers union appeared forgiving and nurturing, trying to salvage a young teacher. In reality, the union had no interest in protecting a non-tenured teacher from an administration that appreciated not having to search for a replacement hire mid-term. It was a simple political maneuver.

The perfect world Alice and I thought we were making became tenuous. We put off the wedding. Right away I stumbled onto the job at Acme-Archer. The controller once taught high school accounting, and the process engineer had taught shop class. They had pity on me and considered a liberal arts education desirable for a job where critical thinking and excellent communication was required. I excelled.

Meanwhile over summer vacation, our friends just began to drift away. Alice and I became more dependent on one another. Our parents both wished we would get married and move back home, but also told us they realized we had to do what we deemed important, and that things worth having are things worth struggling for. That fall, Alice went back to teaching and I was comfortable in my job. I took Columbus Day off because she was out of school. We went rummaging to antique stores for a fainting couch. We bought the most splendidly awful, gaudy, red velvet fainting couch ever made. We labored to get it into our second floor apartment. We dropped it into place and Alice fell into it. Face first in an awful lunging kind of way. We never knew she had an aneurysm until it ruptured. It was fatal.

I thought I was unable to stand with her parents at the viewing, so I refused to attend. I was at her funeral then watched Rich cover up her grave. That night I drove back to Greenfield and went to work the next day, I used Acme-Archer as my big blanket to pull up over my head and protect me from the boogey man the world had become. My illogical mind said that I could never return to Lake Ann and live a happy life since I had so dismally failed at a career and love; two things I perceived as powerful measures of a man.

Over the years I had come to terms with my torturous world. Alice's parents and I learned to like each other, forgive each other and ourselves for our irrational thoughts and feelings relating to the circumstances of the death of their only child.

In fact, I became so engrossed in my life's routine I couldn't conceive of a return to Lake Ann. In the grand scheme of the world, my work was pretty meaningless. It was in fact very dull. Worse, it was important to engineers and others whose careers necessitated that a better performing rubber compound be formulated to withstand even greater meaningless tests and rigors. Furthermore, that it constantly be manufactured to consistency tighter tolerance specifications irrelevant to its physical performance. But all of this was vitally important in order to quantify those improvements thereby leading to pay raises and promotions, and paragraphs of important sounding press for the trade magazines.

So here I was with my dad and sister. I was thinking with that part of a man's brain, when he is driving and gets lost, that causes him to always turn onto dead end roads. But I was speaking with the intuitive part of my brain that I had let sleep until, apparently, my mom's death had caused it to stir and speak up. Innately, our human spirit wants to survive. More so perhaps, thrive. Maybe Lake Ann was where that was to happen.

"Maybe if I show promise for these couple of weeks, I could take 10-12 weeks of my vacation next summer too." I seemed to speak without thinking again. Dad's gaping mouth was grinning. I think I could have stuffed a hard-boiled smoked egg from the deli into Liz's mouth, and she wouldn't have even noticed it. And Liz hated those eggs.

The doorbell rang so I answered it. It was Pastor Brock, she asked if there was anything she could do before the funeral, and if we had any questions or concerns. Dad had her come in and sit down. Then he asked Pastor Brock if they could put the funeral off for a day. Pastor Brock sat expressionless for an instant but blinked as if her mind was scanning some text for the right thing to say.

"It was already in the newspaper Will, the funeral home has everything set. Why would you possibly…" but dad cut her off.

"The old man, Erik Von Rath, we think, you know, maybe a service could include him and Grace." We all were looking at Pastor Brock. She eased back into her chair.

"It would need to be Protestant and Roman Catholic you know? What you are suggesting is a bit unconventional." We all looked at the Pastor, unrelenting in the strength of our conviction that this was the right thing to do. In her last act of living, Mom began to meddle in yet another person's life, never mind that he was already dead. Dad, Liz and I were to finish her uncompleted task of getting to know her newest "friend," a fellow traveler through this adventure of life.

"I'll call Father Joe and the funeral home. Maybe

I should use the phone," Pastor Brock said as she began moving toward it and reaching into her coat pocket for her electronic personal organizer which contained, along with many others, the phone numbers of Father Joe and the funeral home.

The next morning was kind of somber and quiet around the house. Hazel had stopped by with a coffeecake. We made small talk with her for awhile.

"You are going to feel very different at the end of the day." She smiled and patted our heads and shoulders, whatever she could easily reach. Then she got up to leave.

None of us had asked Hazel to explain what she meant, it sounded like a cliché, or taken from inside a fortune cookie. But Hazel was more sincere than that, wiser too. That morning we just weren't in the mood to become wiser. Throughout the visitation hours, individually we all thought about Hazel's words. Later that evening Dad, Liz and I talked about our day. It is an odd custom to be grieving, and still, at the same time required to receive visitors at the funeral home. Earlier that day this loomed a weighty task. But that evening we all agreed that by the end of the day, beyond our physical tiredness, there was an emotional transformation that had taken place. We decided that Hazel had predicted accurately. Each of us had been warmed, or stirred by one person or another who had an especially kind thing to say; a forgotten or unknown incident about Mom that was significant. Of particular impact were the individual sentiments expressed by people that described the magnificent ways in which Mom was uniquely special to them. Equally powerful were handshakes or hugs delivered in silence by people like Rich, who shared and understood our grief without diluting the impact of this knowledge by speaking a word.

The next day, which was supposed to have been the funeral, continued to be eventful. I had gone to Hazel's to visit and return the pan, which yesterday, contained that great coffee cake. Meanwhile Margo had driven up for Mom's funeral, and not finding one, sought out Dad and Liz. She tearfully replied that she had some business the next morning in Indianapolis and that she had already rescheduled it once and felt she must attend. She noted that she felt uncomfortable about not going to the funeral and hoped that Dad and Liz would forgive her. Dad had tried to assure her that she was clearly feeling worse about it than he was, and that he was so glad she had interrupted her moving schedule anyway.

"Margo, Mom was intuitively a good decision maker. Dad and I would have to admit that once again she chose correctly, a friend and a co-worker," Liz said.

Liz had spoken like one of our parents. Employees at Bahle's were considered co-workers. Mom and

Dad were pretty egalitarian in their thinking as it related to status and hierarchy. They believed that in the routine affairs of each day, owners and workers quietly assumed their roles by their actions and their attitudes. Dad always thought that helping them have a sense of ownership created a better employee.

Margo told Dad and Liz that she was so happy to have met Grace that she instantly solved a problem.

"You see, I no longer have any immediate family. Leaving my friends in Indianapolis and moving to Lake Ann, while adventurous, seemed scary and lonely. Knowing Grace even for those few weeks just made all those worries disappear," Margo had said.

"Tomorrow I have some legal matters to tend to. There is a trust I need to deal with, it's how I was able to buy the house," Margo went on, "When I was small my dad died of a heart attack at work. We lived in Kokomo and he was an engineer at GM Delco. He used to tell Mom that she deserved to be a millionaire. At his death, she became one. It was such a big shock to her that she could never even think of another man. I was an only child so Mom and I were alone together until a couple of years ago when she passed on. She was astute with finances, and happily I am the benefactor of that. But boy have I had to learn about the complex world of estate planning! Anyway, you see why I must be in Indianapolis."

Dad urged Margo to stay a bit longer. He made them all drinks and they began to talk and know each other a bit more, Dad, Margo and Liz. I, however, was still at Hazel's, and we were getting some startling details about the late Erik Von Rath.

As I arrived at Hazel's with the empty coffeecake pan, she had just finished a conversation with old Father Joe, inviting him to brunch. "I have been in a baking mood and wondered if you would like some muffins, Father?"

"It is my constant duty to oblige my parishioners," he replied.

Hazel was hanging up the phone as I walked in through the door and spoke to her.

"Hazel, my mom taught me that it was bad manners to return a pan empty, but under the circumstances, I thought you would understand," I said.

"Oh, for Heavens sake Max, I should say so!" Hazel replied. "Now I will tell you what I told your mom many times, that piece of advice on manners is strictly about guilt. So you just put it out of your mind. Max, join Father Joe and me for muffins."

Having walked straight way to the kitchen, I had never looked around. So apologizing I turned and said:

"Oh, Father Joe, I'm sorry." I stopped, perplexed

a bit, not seeing the old Priest anywhere. Hazel patted my head.

"Father Joe will be along soon Maxie boy," She said.

The previous evening had seen Father Joe very busy. His meeting with the police chief and coroner had lasted not quite halfway through the bottle of scotch. The state people helping with the investigation as well as a local sheriff's reservist found the chief at the Clubhouse to update him.

"Chief, it looks like everything he owned was in that car. Luggage full of clothes, shoes, some hand tools, and a few books, its weird," the reservist reported.

Soon after a state police trooper suggested to the chief they speak in private. The chief rebutted.

"Father Joe has essential information on this case. We've been piecing it together, the coroner, Father Joe and I."

"See son, Father Joe here knew the deceased." He said this looking the state trooper in the eye and pulled a chair out for him at the same time. The officer sat, not sure whether he was being invited or instructed to do so. Drink glasses were empty and the bottle sat still as the priest, coroner and the chief told the details and spoke their theories. Satisfied with its telling, there came a pause. Excitedly the state trooper's eyes darted from one person to another.

"Then you're gonna love this. First, maybe we should toast the speedy success of this investigation. Consider me off duty of course."

"How about a glass for our friend here," the chief hollered to Billie. She was there in an instant, her frail frame moved quickly and quietly. She was such a part of the place that you hardly noticed her.

"Mind?" She asked after pouring their four glasses then holding one of her own out before them.

"By all means! But please, allow me," the priest requested as he took the bottle from her and poured some into her glass.

"Thanks," Billie responded and took her place behind the bar.

"There was a lot of print material in the metal box. Some we couldn't make out, some we could. There were pictures, and some recipe cards wrapped in plastic bags with rubber bands all over the place. We found a cashier's check and some stock certificates." The listeners all began to move in their chairs.

"That wouldn't seem unusual if you were moving. Was the cashier's check made out to himself? He was probably going to deposit it all at a bank here," the coroner asserted.

"Yes, the cashier's check was in the name of Erik Von Rath, and I suspect you are right," said the trooper.

"Father, I think you should locate any and all

correspondence you still may have. Correspondence you had with the deceased. Did anyone witness discussions the two of you had, perhaps, when he came to visit?" the trooper continued.

"There were no visits or discussions, son. We corresponded simply like people of a shared faith, one seeking to find a new and suitable vocation in which to exercise his faith, the other simply to facilitate it."

"Father, you never met the deceased? I think this is odd," the trooper mentioned.

"He was an old German man of immigrant parents. Erik thought that we might have met once at the retreat center here. After Vatican II he came for a deacon's workshop. Although I was serving in Fort Wayne at that time, I had attended many retreats at Lake Ann."

"He wrote initially to the retreat center at Lake Ann. It just so happened that I have been serving the community for some time and was therefore recipient of his letters," Father Joe noted.

"Well, that's not all you're recipient to Father. I'm a state trooper not a lawyer, but I think the deceased's intentions were very clear." "I own a few shares of G.E. stock, myself. Rubber-banded and wrapped in plastic were 500 shares owned by Erik Von Rath."

"Well bless his soul!" Father Joe hoisted his glass.

"The shares were bought 50 at a time beginning in the late 50's through the 60's. I made a call to confirm my hunch. Adjusting for splits you see, those 500 shares now represent 48,000 shares." "This is a couple of million bucks, Father."

"Blessed Joseph and Mary." "Are you certain of this?" quizzed the old priest.

"Pretty sure!" the young trooper declared.

The coroner and the chief just shook their heads in disbelief. "This is gonna be the stuff of coffee talk for a long, long time," the coroner smiled as she spoke.

Hazel's doorbell rang. It was Father Joe. "You needed some help breaking muffins, my dear?" He almost seemed sincere.

"Come in Father. Max Bahle is joining us too."

We ate muffins and listened to the priest recount details from his previous evening's meeting at the Clubhouse. Father Joe thanked Hazel and declared, "Pastor Brock and I have much to do by tomorrow."

"As do we ladies, Father!" She referred of course to the church dinner following the funeral, a joint dinner by Roman Catholics and Lutherans. Certain to be a cook-off competition between congregations, it could only end in a judging draw as the combined experience of hundreds and hundreds of years from among dozens of women would, slice by slice, spoon by spoon, yield one flawless serving after another.

By the time I returned to dad's house, Margo had left. Dad and Liz were amazed with the details I reported to them from the investigation, as told by the old priest, just as I had been.

"What the? That sounds like a motorcycle." Dad got up to look out a window onto the driveway. Touching my arm in order to be sure she had my attention, Liz said, "yer kinfolk is here."

CHAPTER 2
THE FUNERAL

Uncle Wayne and Aunt Bert lived in the southern part of Indiana near the Ohio River, at the edge of the Hoosier National Forrest. Their only son, Wayne junior, lived with them. Uncle Wayne's father and my mother's father were brothers. So I think Uncle Wayne was my great uncle, and Wayne junior a second cousin – actually such matters have always been confusing, and are for many people. In at least one instance this confusion was highlighted in our family.

Wayne junior who was quite a bit older than me, and a few years older than Liz, had more or less developed what was sometimes referred to as "an eye" for Liz. She recounted how Wayne junior stopped by one Saturday early in the summer that she had graduated from high school. He confessed that he "fancied" her and he "thought he'd like to marry her, so perhaps they should begin courtin'." Realizing that Wayne junior was both dimwitted and serious,

Liz chose her approach. "Wayne junior, I'm so flattered! The thing is, in school we learned that it is illegal to marry your cousin – and your babies might be imbeciles."

If the truth were known, Wayne junior may have been an unwitting participant in just such a biological legacy. The backwoods of rural southern Indiana from which Aunt Bert came may have involved some first cousin unions. Such speculation occurred only rarely in private family conversation that didn't include Aunt Bert or the two Waynes. But it resulted as conversation because Aunt Bert would sometimes refer to one of her relatives unknown to us. Then, in her rapid fire approach to talking, she would blister us with genealogical connectedness that we couldn't really follow, but gave us the notion that there were many same named persons in her heritage, or, well, just not so many branches on the family tree.

So cousin Wayne junior, Liz's dejected suitor, thanked her for informing him of such matters, confessed his embarrassment and never mentioned his wish again.

Quickly, Liz and I suggested to dad that our guests could use my old room, and Liz's. I'd sleep on the couch and Liz would impose on a friend from work, or Hazel.

We walked outside to greet our relatives, Wayne junior and his mom – our Aunt Bert. We had understood that Uncle Wayne seldom traveled. He was very busy with his work of passion. He broke mules to harness, and trained them to pull stone sleds. Mechanized equipment was prohibited from use in the Hoosier National Forest, so the work of trail management and maintenance was done by man and beast. Uncle Wayne and his mules were somewhat legendary among those who worked hauling gravel to fill washouts, or towing fallen logs from paths. In terms of more family gossip, what was legend to us was that Uncle Wayne's best drinking pal was likely an old mule named Sal.

Wayne junior stretched after he got off his motorcycle. Then he went to the sidecar which carried Aunt Bert and Skipper. He grabbed Skipper so Aunt Bert could wrestle herself free from the confines of the sidecar. Skipper was a homely, tiny dog of unknown breed that had huge bulging eyes. I walked over to Wayne junior and petted Skipper, held in his arms, before, I had to endure Aunt Bert pointing one of her thin, crooked fingers my way and saying – "Now get over there and say hi to Skipper." Petting Skipper I smiled while Aunt Bert pointed to dad and Liz and beckoned, "Git on over there and say hi to Skipper!"

Behind his motorcycle, Wayne junior towed a tiny homemade trailer which carried their suitcases. He removed only one, and announced that he was, "gonna look up Rich Franken, and maybe bunk with him."

One summer, apparently before the mule training was a big endeavor, Uncle Wayne, Aunt Bert, and Wayne junior summered at a cottage on Lake Ann. Rich was at that time a groundskeeper at a nearby public golf course, and got Wayne junior a summer job there. They also golfed together. No one knew if their activities were to mock the different people who may have spoke down to them, or if they were just a couple of simple wild bucks following their imaginations in the pursuit of fun. The two were seen from time to time golfing at night. They wore miner's hats and so did their "caddy." Their caddy was a fully-body mannequin fastened to their golf cart. It was female. It had a blond wig. It wore a green polka-dot bikini. I was old enough that she made an impression on me. I hoped that when I had a girlfriend, that she would wear a green polka-dot bikini. The boy's mannequin seemed friendly, sort of posing in a permanent waving posture, and smiling conservatively. She had a surgery, which was performed by Rich and Wayne junior. It left her with a rather large and unattractive hole in her back, but was necessary in order to hold their clubs – both of them. Not too serious about their sport, they shared the two clubs. One "a fat one" was found by Rich at the public course hanging out of a tree. It had apparently been placed there by someone who had a little trouble with their game that day. The second "a skinny one" was "lifted" when one or the other, perhaps both, simply abandoned their putt-putt miniature golf outing when a thunderstorm struck.

Their nocturnal sport seemed harmless enough and few people complained. Some of course, found it humorous.

"Rich's phone number is on a list stuck on the side of the refrigerator. Phone's on the wall beside it." Dad instructed Wayne junior. Dad had very recently scanned the list himself, and called Rich. He wondered how many times to come would such simple things remind him of mom's death.

"So sorry about Grace," Aunt Bert said, but to no one in particular.

"Max, Lizzie, so sorry about your mom. Uncle Will, so sorry about Aunt Grace," Wayne junior spoke softly. He handed a trembling Skipper to Aunt Bert. "Why you're cold you little shit, ain't ye?"

Wayne junior emerged from the house and announced that he would be heading off to see Rich and would bunk there.

"Come back for dinner, bring Rich along. We've got so much food here – it's unbelievable," urged Dad.

Liz and I took that instant to spar a bit, if only through facial gestures and eye contact: who would get to leave and who would stay in the house with dad and Aunt Bert was the question we both had. Liz took the upper hand. "Max can sleep on the couch. Aunt Bert can have his room tonight." Then walking toward me whispered in a punctuated, staccato rhythm, "neither-you-or-I-can leave dad tonight." And she strode to the house.

Eventually and fortunately, Rich and Wayne junior returned for supper. But with Rich along, another guest to entertain, Aunt Bert was in rare form. We learned why she believed amusement parks and carnival rides with all their fancy moving lights would lure UFOs to the earth. We learned that she couldn't approve of airline travel, even though she had recently flown. Aunt Bert believed that quickly crossing all those time zones would shorten your life.

She told of her trip to Los Angeles with Wayne junior just recently in fact. She enters a lot of sweepstakes and won a trip. Wayne junior escorted his mother. They saw the "Tonight Show." "We got in line after lunch. They record that show. It's made in the afternoon, did you know that?"

Eventually and unfortunately, Rich and Wayne junior called it a night and left.

Then it was time for Aunt Bert to go into her story: "Poor Wayne junior Born with his tongue grown to the bottom of his mouth. Had to get it cut loose with an operation. Why, that tongue's too big for his mouth," I said to the doctor. "If you watch he kinda rolls that tongue around and sorta chews it I guess."

With a bold-face lie, dad said the only thing you could say in such a situation: "I really never noticed."

We probably never noticed his incessant habit of jingling his loose change in his pocket with his hand either.

"Bert, I think it's time we all went to bed," spoke dad. "Tomorrow's the funeral."

Wayne junior arrived back at the house quite early. Dad and Liz stayed in their rooms. I pretended to sleep until Aunt Bert had gotten up and took Skipper out to "do his job." Noisily she returned and began to make coffee and toast. Eventually we all filled in around the table and no one had much to say, except of course Aunt Bert. Oddly, whatever it may have been that she wanted to talk about, on that morning she had the good judgment to speak very little.

"I'll just leave you all be awhile," Aunt Bert spoke as she scooped up little Skipper and returned to her room. We looked at Wayne junior. He blinked several times and seemed to have mesmerized himself by rolling his tongue around in his mouth. Dad looked at Liz and I, then said, "I was visited last night. At the foot of my bed, I woke up and sensed someone there. I couldn't make anyone out in the dark you know. But I sensed it was your mom." Liz and I looked at him blankly. Thankfully Wayne junior was there. "What did Aunt Grace – bless her soul – have to say Uncle Will?"

"She liked what I told the preacher," dad smiled. Tears began to flow down his face, but through a faint smile he spoke: "I have had a great life kids. Look at the two of you. I'm so proud of you both. I have had work that I enjoyed all these years. I have had health. I have wonderful friends and loyal customers. In all this, I still have your mom. This will carry me through." Liz got up wiping tears from her cheeks and threw her arms around dad as she bent over him. I went over and briefly touched them both. Then I went into the living room, to my suitcase for some fresh clothes which I carried into the bathroom. Skipper came running from somewhere and Wayne junior picked him up and knocked on his mother's door.

Finally we were all ready to go. Skipper was shut in the bathroom. Dad and Liz rode together. Aunt Bert and Wayne junior went together. He drove Liz's car. I wanted to drive by myself. I couldn't explain why, but no one demanded an explanation either.

We arrived at St. Paul's Lutheran Church and were seated in the front row. Aunt Bert and Wayne junior were behind us.

The two caskets, the Lutheran minister, and the Roman Catholic priest were all evidence that this was my mother's funeral. It wasn't going to be exactly like all others.

Pastor Brock began: "Whether Grace Bahle's spirit was yet with her as she slipped through the water I cannot say. But she would use her body to introduce us to Erik Von Rath. We may never have known how special he was, had she not introduced us. Most of us here have at one time or another been recipient of her warmth, generosity and genuine concern. I recently asked Will, if perhaps he or Grace had any pearls of wisdom. He explained that in his younger days he wanted to be in charge and be noticed; to do something important and always be remembered for it. 'Don't you want that too?' He had asked. Grace then told her young husband that she wakes up everyday loving the man she chose to marry, and knowing that she was loved in return. She had children she adored. She was proud to carry on a trade and business taught to them by his father. She chose to love the life she had. The young couple decided that day to adopt the same philosophical framework in order to guide them together through their lives. The young wife urged her husband to adopt her frame of reference. And what Will has gleaned from these years, he summed up for me the other day. 'What will sustain me is realizing that my success is the life and love we gave to one another. It is enough in this world because our hearts and minds alone – no one else's – measured how rich and full our life together has been.'

"I would add," continued Pastor Brock, "that the irony in living seems to be how effective you become in touching the lives of others without that being the goal.

"As surely as Grace Bahle will be missed, let us remember that she was blessed by this family of hers, this congregation of hers, this community of hers, to be a blessing to this family, this congregation, and this community. Blessed to be a blessing. Amen."

Pastor Brock sat down and Father Joe stood and began to speak: "Please meet Erik Von Rath. An old man I may have met many years ago here at Lake Ann, on retreat. A man who in his advancing years began to correspond with me. He described how as a young man he would have chosen the monastery, but instead chose to honor his mother and father and work in their tiny bakery. After his parents were gone, and he retired, it occurred to him to use his baking talents and immerse himself in the atmosphere of the church by moving to Lake Ann and living at the retreat center. He only asked for room and board, and he would, in exchange, bake bread. He arrived during the last great blizzard. Private and simple he seemed to vanish without anyone noticing. Quite a contrast to Grace Bahle. Erik Von Rath lived with quiet purpose even though he never lived the monastic life he earlier had desired. He was a caregiver to his parents, and honored their legacy in their community by operating their bakery until he became elderly. In this he honored God."

"Erik Von Rath's honor for his faith will live on. It was his intent to leave his estate to the church. Ironically, this man has left a gift that will cause us to acknowledge him and remember him even though he was unknown to us. I am struck at how two different people have shown us these different ways to save ourselves from the plague infecting modern man's sense of self: boredom and desperation. It would appear that what we are here for, the purpose of our birth, is simply to honor life; beginning with our own by growing a passion to be a good person among all people."

Alter boys assisted in preparing the incensor; the priest blessed the body, and the sanctuary. We were led out into waiting cars for the trip to the cemetery. As we arrived at the cemetery we observed two prepared burial sites, although some distance apart. One belonged to Erik Von Rath, the other to mom. It was easy to be distracted from our graveside service and watch the priest attended by a couple of parishioners quickly finish their service of laying Erik Von Rath to rest. It was easy because I needed distraction. I felt barely strong enough to manage my own grief, but the intense sorrow of some of Mom's friends was of no help to assist us with our own, and their weeping weighed intensely on our emotional shoulders in those somber moments at the grave. Finally, we filed back into the cars to return to the church for a lunch.

As I looked out the window of the car as we pulled away, Rich pulled a flower from inside his vest. He threw it into Mom's grave. The vault truck began to move into place and Rich, as he had many, many times before, sealed the grave of someone's wife, someone's mother and someone's friend.

CHAPTER 3
MARGO

The next two weeks came and went before I knew it. I was with dad all day, everyday, and spent the evenings with him as well. At least once a day I saw Liz at the store, but it was the evenings at dad's that were magical; the three of us sitting up late into the night getting reacquainted. Without recognizing it as work, we began to re-weave the fabric of our lives together without Mom's actual presence, but constantly noting ways in which she had influenced our individual persons, and the family we had become.

As dad and I struggled to get the store running smoothly, taking care of those tasks that Mom always had done, we discovered that we enjoyed working together. Customers responded favorably, too. Dad hadn't spent much time waiting on the counter in recent years, and seemed exhilarated by the kindness of his customers. His public lavished over him so much that he even became somewhat of a stage act. During a busy stint one Saturday he brought a pan of pork chops to the case which I had earlier cut: he held them up and said, "These are pork chops, in case you couldn't tell. They are five-eights of an inch thick. These are cut by Max – just like I've taught him."

They didn't look exactly like dad's chops, and everyone knew it, including me. As I started to cut them, I got a wrong angle on the loin butt. Each chop appeared to have an oversized bone in it. Meat cutting, like billiards, has its finesse in geometry.

So Dad's announcement was his way of apologizing to his customers and promising to return to his usual high standards. But it also meant, "This is my son. He's doing the best he can. Buy the chops or don't. What we don't need right now is criticism."

Dad seemed to have an energy for being entertaining – even shocking. On one occasion he carried the entire half carcass of a lamb out of the cooler to cut a special order from it while the customer waited. As he emerged from the cooler, he hoisted the lamb over one shoulder and with precision timing and as carefully as a good comedian with his cue, placed his free hand to his head as a gesture for forgetfulness and exclaimed, "Oh dear! This is that greyhound!" He trudged back into the cooler, emerging moments later with her order, which apparently he had cut immediately following her earlier phone call to the store. Actually, it was pretty funny. I hadn't remembered how slender a once wooly lamb's carcass looks. How much its shape or profile looks like a big, short-haired dog. I joined in with dad's performances, "I'm sticking to beef here on out!" I announced, and with a carving knife punctuating the air above my head, said, "It's harder to mistake." Dad laughed. We were having some time, he and I.

After work, at home he was just as surprising, but seriously so. He, Liz, and I were in the sunroom watching a sunset one evening. He said, "Your mom and I loved this lake, this place. People used to row boats out and float around. Just sit and look. Sit and talk. Read. Nowadays they zoom. It's movement, motion, speed and noise. I think people are afraid to talk to themselves, look at themselves inside. I think they are addicted to their adrenalin. Anyway, that's a change me and your mom noticed over the years."

Liz and I looked at him, listened to him in amazement.

We really hadn't heard Dad speak like this. Maybe it was because mom always had so much to say. But it was great. We knew that dad had more strength and more passion for life than we realized.

It seemed like a good opportunity to bring it up, so before I thought it over much, or carefully chose my words, I just blurted, "So do you think Grandma and Grandpa's old apartment above the store could be fixed up?"

"What for?" Dad seemed curious.

"Me. That is, if I have a job at the store." He stood up in front of me with outstretched arms. I stood up and he hugged me. He quivered, my neck felt wet. He began to sob. He was happy and approved, well, was overjoyed with my decision; and request. But he continued to sob, I glanced at Liz, she nodded approvingly and wiped tears from her face. Tears of grief and joy came from the same well spring. Dad had tapped into it. Liz and I believed that it was necessarily uncomfortable, and recognized not a weakness, but, a strength in our dad. In time, he was going to be just fine.

Following the funeral, my two weeks with Dad went by quickly. When I returned to Greenfield to work and to my apartment, I returned changed. My apartment didn't feel like home. Greenfield didn't feel like my town. Additionally, the Acme Archer Company hadn't folded up in my absence. Orders were shipping incomplete and short. Problems with raw materials and orders in process had clobbered my clean perpetual inventory. Things weren't perfect, but they worked. This knowledge and realization was for my sanity a good thing but for my ego – well, not so-good. I worked hard and long hours amending computer records to actual production inventories. I was usually in the office by 7:00 a.m. and didn't leave until 9:00 or 10:00 p.m. But I called Dad and Liz everyday.

Liz continued to ask if I had resigned. Liz and I usually spoke during the day knowing we could reach one another at work. Her schedule was fairly routine; Monday, Wednesday, and Friday mornings at the animal clinic and two full days at the hospital. She alternated Tuesday- Thursdays and Saturday-Sundays.

We used to e-mail each other and would seemingly "play tag" with the voice mail features on our home and cellular telephones. At her urging, we abandoned all of that and kept our home answering machines only. What started out as time management tools ended up being stressors. Liz called this the paradox in the lure to be constantly connected to communication. Liz was unafraid to jump into new technologies and trends. But she understood herself well enough to know that she maintained sanity by finding ways to be quiet and simplify her life where she could. I agreed. She meditated and practiced yoga. I read and attempted to be contemplative. Different paths, same purpose, we agreed.

One day as we spoke Liz asked, "So what do you think you'll miss once you have left Greenfield?"

Her question seemed easy enough to answer because I so looked forward to being back in Lake Ann. Everyday there were occurrences that made me realize that either emotionally or intellectually, in certain ways I had already gone back home.

"Nothing." I stated flatly. "I won't miss a thing about Greenfield." But before I finished that statement I realized that there was something I would miss. "Wait!" I was emphatic. "Bucky Wong's!"

"Is that the little Chinese restaurant you took the folks and me to a couple years back? Next door to the crematorium?" Liz wanted to know.

"Yeah, that was Bucky Wong's."

"Gross, Max." And with that Liz implied that indeed there was nothing I should miss about Greenfield.

Bucky Wong's was a small Chinese restaurant not far from where I worked. It was located in an area more industrial than retail, and was in fact, next door to a crematorium. Bucky, was of course, not the proprietor's real name. Neither was Wong. He chose Wong because he considered it intelligent marketing. His legal name had about fourteen letters in it, two of which were vowels. But he loved the name Bucky. It seemed very American to him. Anyway, that was his opinion from seeing some old American Westerns on television. Bucky, his wife, and their daughter were from the nation of Laos.

His wife and child had lived in a refugee camp in Thailand hoping for his release from a North Vietnamese prisoner of war camp. Somehow Bucky managed to survive his ordeal and eventually escape. I say survive because malnourishment and disease claimed the lives of many of his fellow captives. He believed that he survived and kept strong enough for his eventual escape by drinking his own urine.

Once reunited with his family in Thailand, they were assisted by a group of Mennonites who arranged for Bucky and his family to immigrate to the United States. They settled in, of all places, Greenfield, Indiana. Bucky recalls stepping off the airliner in Chicago and noticing a big man in a cowboy hat. The man noticed him too, and said; "Howdy there Bucky." To which Bucky replied in his best English: "Howdy partner."

The man was most likely a red neck, not a cowboy, and probably made reference to Bucky's rather enormous eye-teeth. But ironically Bucky felt welcomed and legitimatised at the same time. Ever since hearing that story I was convinced that as long as. Bucky felt good about it, why would I want to make an issue of it? After all, I wasn't at the airport. The man just may have been an honest-to-goodness, kind-hearted cowboy.

Bucky was charming and industrious. His wife and daughter seemed to talk ceaselessly. They all laughed and touched each other often. They were a pleasure to be around. I confess that I was terribly amused with certain of Bucky's words when he spoke. Sometimes, late, I would be their final patron. Bucky would sit and talk with me. He would usually announce that he; "must go back to 'chicken' and get to work." He referred of course to the kitchen. But I loved to hear him say it his way.

In his early years in business he had some problems with the health inspector. He couldn't make himself use trashcan liners. A frugal man, he thought the idea of buying something for the express purpose of throwing it away was akin to insanity.

He was also one of the most patriotic people I had known. Every morning he raised the American flag on the pole mounted diagonally on the front of his building. Every evening he slowly lowered it, carefully carried it inside the restaurant, and dutifully and respectfully folded it.

I saw Bucky more than once a week usually. I told Liz that I would miss Bucky Wong's. I would miss the man and his family. And I would miss their cashew chicken.

Dad kept saying how glad he would be when I moved back home. He remarked each time we spoke, "Hey, that Margo is somethin' else. We're lucky she came along."

Gradually, I had production running like a well-greased machine again. One Friday morning I looked out my window and saw the company president arrive in his car. I met him at the door and asked if we could chat. I handed him some safety glasses and said, "Let's take a walk." My strategy was that we would walk through the plant, and as we moved from one area to another the commotion would assist us with the uncomfortable silence between us as I announced my resignation. He handled it well. In fact, suggesting that, "If he were me, he would do the same thing." By mid morning, in our regular staff meeting, I had announced that I would be leaving in a month. I left early that day, and drove to Lake Ann and stopped in at the store. I spoke awhile to Dad and told him that I'd see him after the store closed, at his house.

Meanwhile, I needed to get to the lumber yard and talk about some things I needed to get delivered to my new apartment above the store which I hoped to make habitable over the next few months. There weren't any customers in the store at the time and Dad went into the back to clean up the bandsaw, and the meat grinder. I was famished and grabbed one of the pre-packaged sandwiches from the case. As I headed for the front door I heard a voice unknown to me from the side of the store, from an emergency fire safety door that was not for use by the public. Mom used to come and go through that door when she needed to make bank deposits. She parked in the side lot. "Hey Bub – you pay for that sandwich?" The female voice demanded to know. I froze in the doorway. Those words were shocking, paradoxically, I was being accused in that moment of shoplifting, yet, I had never in my entire life paid for anything that I ate or carried out of my parent's store. I felt flushed and sweaty nonetheless. I turned around, she slowly approached me. "Margo?" I sheepishly asked, not sure who else it could be, yet not quite thinking that she looked like my mental picture of someone named Margo. "You're Margo right? But you don't look like a Margo." I blurted out. Sure that I was visibly sweating, I felt like peeing in my pants. Her eyes were big and brown and round. She had long dark lashes like a doe deer, I thought. They blinked almost in slow motion, she drew nearer. "I'll pay for the sandwich if you like," I said. When recounted to my dad, that statement in the situation described provided him with one of his greatest laughs. He probably told everyone he knew. For years when I'd see the police chief he'd begin, "Pilfered any sandwiches of late Max?"

"So what's a Margo supposed to look like?" She stopped a few feet from me. Her gaze fixed on me, serious but not hostile or angry.

"I'm sorry, I swear I don't know why I said… I'm Max." I extended my hand.

At once she flushed, and said, "Oh my god, I'm sorry," and reached to take my hand. The bank deposit bags slipped off the top of the stack of mail and everything went on the floor. She knelt down. "I'm sorry, I should have known." She seemed to be talking to the scattered pile formerly in order in her arms. I knelt down, sure that this was Margo, but for some reason, only understood by my heart, needed to hear her say it. "Yes, I'm Margo." Those eyes met mine. "Now, do I seem like a Margo to you?" She seemed apologetic. I couldn't speak but shook my head no.

"Margo, I have to go to the lumberyard – I'm having a late lunch." I held up the sandwich. "I've got to go." I handed her the few items I gathered up for her. I headed down the street in a daze. Suddenly, I realized that the sandwich had slipped out of my hand. Stopping, I noticed it wasn't directly near by. Also, I realized that I had wandered a few yards down the street, opposite the direction of the lumberyard, and, most interestingly, I had forgotten to take my car. I tried to compose myself, I began to jog back to the car, hoping no one was watching or noticing what I was doing. *Get ahold of yourself! You're acting like a pie-eyed junior high schooler! I thought to myself. Thank goodness, I thought, soon I'll be talking drywall board and paint with the boys at the lumberyard.*

Later, on the way back to Dad's house I began to wonder how I was going to conduct myself and settle down when I started full time at the store, now that Margo was there. She was to me, arresting and captivating.

Dad and Liz were home when I got there. The boys at the lumberyard wanted to toast a few in honor of the occasion of my, soon-to-be, return to Lake Ann.

Over the next few weeks, we toasted the occasion many, many times.

Opening the door, dad was laughing, "Why here's that deli sandwich thief, Liz." Immediately he was reminded of something else. Serious and puzzled he announced to no one in particular, more like thinking out loud, "On my way home I swear I ran over a whole sandwich along the street – just a few feet from the store. What the hell was that about?"

"Come in, come in – I'm starved. Let's make some supper," he said.

Dad put some ground beef patties in the electric countertop grill. Liz poured some couscous into a pan of boiling water on the stove and handed me a bowl of coleslaw to put on the table.

"Margo asked if she could come by tonight. Bring a red velvet cake! I said," dad spoke as the hamburgers sizzled.

"Well dad!" Liz began, "I was kidding," he said.

"But does poor Margo know that? Are you like that at work all day with her?" Liz continued.

"You met her yet Max?" Liz asked.

"Um, yeah. Sure did. Seems nice." I had my head

in the refrigerator looking for mustard, ketchup and sweet relish.

We finished eating and it was about dark. Cicada bugs were singing loudly outside. Someone was banging on the screen door. "I'll get it," Liz moved toward the door.

"Hi Margo. Welcome. Oh dear, you've got cake. Now listen – you've got to learn when dad is pulling your chain."

As they headed into the kitchen Margo said, "Well I've never had red velvet cake so I looked it up in my favorite cookbook: A Recipe for Damned Near Everything," she mused. A boxed cake mix, some red food coloring, cup of mayonnaise, half-hour in my little easy bake oven – viola!"

"Of course, the frosting is tofu," Margo spoke wryly to Liz, but for dad's benefit – this time she would pull his chain.

"Oh no. I don't want bean curd. I sell meat. We can't have tofu here."

As dad spoke Margo patted his back, "There, there, I put lard in it too," she smiled.

"Hi Max."

"Hello, again, Margo," I blushed.

Liz cocked her head looking first at me, then Margo, then back to me. Her pursed lips curved into a smile and she arched one eyebrow. Liz didn't miss a single detail in relationship dynamics it seemed.

Confident, if not cocky, at having keyed in on some new and exciting element unfolding in someone else's life, she spun around to get plates, forks and a cake knife. Margo had sat across from me. Dad was serving coffee.

It was getting late. The four of us talked about a great many things. It seemed that I couldn't disclose much that Margo didn't know something about: where I worked, my deceased fiancé, my brief teaching career. This was clearly the work of Dad, Liz and before them – Mom.

"So you came to the lake when you were a little girl?" I asked Margo. "Yeah." "And now lucky enough to be able to buy a lake home here. So now I have my castle."

"Oh, so now Margo, are you looking for a knight on a white steed?" Liz playfully asked.

"Well, not looking really. You know what? One summer I met him, here at Lake Ann," Margo began, "Some girls I played with had gotten sno-cones. Remember that stand on the beach? And we ran along the street and some of them crossed the street to the parking lot but I didn't because the asphalt was real hot. We laughed and hollered back and forth. Then a boy about our age pulled up on his sting-ray bike with a white banana seat and asked if I needed a ride. He took me painlessly and safely across the street. I guess he was my knight on a white steed."

"Hey, I gave a little girl a ride across the road once. But it wasn't a real sting-ray. It was the Montgomery Ward version. When she hopped off, her sno-cone spilled all over. I thought she was going to cry – so I offered her mine and as she looked at me and reached for it all the other girls said, 'Eew! Max Bahle likes'"–

"Grape," Margo solemnly and softly spoke.

"That was you?" I asked.

"You!" she exclaimed.

Dad clapped and hollered "Oh boy – here we go kids."

Liz was leaning back in her chair just taking it all in, seeming to really enjoy the development.

We were young,middle-aged people, yet barely able to anymore than glance nervously at each other's blushing faces.

"Wow! Hey, I've got to work tomorrow, so I need to skee-daddle!" Margo announced.

"I'll show you out." I spoke quietly as I stood up.

"Hey you two – I'll tell you like I tell the young kids that help in the summer. There's no butt grabbing behind the deli or meat counter!" Dad was so amused with this, he waved as he got up and walked back the hall to his room.

"Hurry back Maxie – we gotta clean up this kitchen yet." Liz smiled.

I walked Margo to her car.

"I feel like I'm 12 again," she said.

"Um, 14, for me."

"See you in a few hours." I spoke, then stood and watched her taillights disappear into the street ahead. Liz pretty well had the kitchen in order but wanted to be sure not to miss the earliest possible chance to sing-song, "Maxie's got a girlfriend." She handed me a little wine. We stood along the counter.

"So what was the point of listing for Margo 'Max's top ten dating disasters'?" I asked.

"Well, Margo has long hair, that one girl had long hair, at least until you shut it in the car door. Then of course, if she ever sits beside you and turns to speak at just the right instant as you put your arm around her – she could get a black eye. Just like that one girl. I like Margo. I'm just trying to forewarn her." Liz teased. "Well, that's why I had to tell about how you would wreck your bike when your big-ol' bell bottoms would tangle on the bike chain."

"OK OK," she said raising her glass, "truce."

"Truce." I clanged my glass to hers.

Back in Greenfield the search for my replacement at Acme-Archer hadn't produced a suitable candidate until my last week. Meanwhile, someone from the data processing department of the company was sent down to observe and document procedurally those tasks which I performed. Mostly he observed. Anyway, now someone else in the company seemed to understand what raw information I put in, and what the resulting data meant and to whom it was relevant on a daily and sometimes hour by hour basis.

Gradually, I had packed and moved many things to my apartment-in-progress in Lake Ann. I was anxious to be there and sometimes would drive there evenings after work only to unload my car and return. One night I surprised Liz and Margo who had entered my apartment and were painting the living room a "nice earthy beige" color. I was of course delighted and surprised until the ladies confessed that their efforts weren't altogether altruistic, but had a sense of urgency to assuring that it wouldn't be painted forest green as I had at some point mentioned. So rather than merciful workers of assistance, they were more like the decorating police. Interrogated in the shadowy painter's lights about my furnishing intentions, I quickly diffused what was a mounting case of rigged justice: I recognized that I had little of interest in household furnishings. I would sell or give away all furnishings and replace them when I moved. Asserting myself I demanded that I keep a platform rocker and parlor lamp that belonged to Grandma and Grandpa Bahle. "Consider that those pieces will be coming home," I arrogantly urged.

I was serious. I was sentimental. A sense of family history was important to me even though I had no children or nieces or nephews to pass heirlooms or information to. I had learned that we Bahle's had been Quakers. Formerly they referred to themselves as "friends." One of our ancestors had been an assistant to Governor Penn. They were pacifists and found the civil war a difficult experience. Wealthy conscientious objectors could hire someone to serve in their stead. One of our ancestors was a poor frontier farmer who deserted his post. He eventually returned to his unit, was wounded, and then was discharged. Matters of conscious it appears, nearly always create conflict, and sometimes suffering. It seems that death is inevitable, so a person may as well live a life guided by some legitimate set of principals in order to own some pride and self-respect. Anyway, that is what struck me as I learned about my ancestors.

There was little fanfare on my last day. I declined earlier attempts at going away get-togethers, but realized, finally, that I needed to close an important chapter in the story of my life.

I informed the president that I was leaving at 2 p.m. to have a drink with the men and women foremen who had labored with me over the years. Most were bourbon drinkers, some got a bit weepy. But June Brighton, who was my surrogate mother, was very encouraging and happy for me.

I had quite a history with June. One autumn I had a fever and difficulty getting out of a chair and straightening up. She repeatedly told me to see a doctor. I thought I had the flu and a backache. I thought pain management was a mind-over-matter issue. But the pain got worse and in the middle of the night I drove myself to the Emergency room of the hospital. Although I don't recall anything about it, I understand that I drove right to the door, got out, and left the car running. I must have been in shock. What I do remember is the attending physician not being too busy as he awaited the lab test results. I assumed his specialty and interest was proctology, because I received an uncomfortable and annoying exam. I recall this because when the surgeon was called in to confer, he too donned a rubber glove. When I protested that the other guy had already been there, the surgeon replied; "you don't want me to take his word for it do you?" I must have ruined his evening's sleep and pissed him off but good to have received such exemplary care.

Mom and Dad were called and arrived about the time I was coming to in my room after the surgery. Mom told how a nurse came in and addressed my roommate by saying, as she snapped her rubber glove on, "time to check your prostate." Mom didn't know what happened exactly, but I became immediately alert and attempted to get out of bed.

What had happened is that my appendix had burst possibly a few days earlier. I was pretty ripe with infection and hospitalized for about a week. Mom didn't stay although she thought she should. I actually enjoyed the quiet and the respite from work. However I needed to remain home a few days until the wick which stuck out of my incision fell out, a sign that it had finished draining the infection.

June would stop by after work and run errands for me. She brought me a computer from work so that I could do what I could to keep things running smoothly. One afternoon she stopped by and I wanted to show her where the wick had finally fallen out. She thought the incision looked red. I thought so too. It seemed warm and kind of hard I thought. As I was pressing around it, it burst open. I fainted. I came around quickly and June took me back to the hospital. In a couple of days, I was home again. But that time a bit depressed with the whole recovery process. As the days went by, June noticed that I wasn't shaving. Then one day she came in while I was finishing an entire box of one of those sugary kid's cereals, you know, with all the bright colored shapes, and all of those great flavors. She asked if I had eaten the box at one setting. I confessed that I had. She looked at me sternly then said; "Max. It's time to come back to work." I considered my debt to June enormous.

Finally, I bid them all well. As I drove away from Greenfield and my friends at Acme-Archer, I began thinking about my new life as a businessman and butcher in Lake Ann. I was feeling philosophical and somber. I thought about Mom's drowning. I thought about my own Christian baptism when I was small, before we were Lutherans. Mine was a fundamentalist type of over forward and over backward total immersion kind of baptism. Anyway, the idea of drowning from one life to emerge into another as reborn seemed to occupy my mind for most of the drive home. Even as I thought about Margo, I wondered if I was drowning in the experience of being in love. Just months ago I never thought it would happen again. It felt like a free-fall. I had no anxiety, no fears. I wasn't struggling against it. I thought I could be reborn into a life with her that would be more fulfilling than my life alone. The kind of fulfillment that comes in return from first giving my total self and love; as selflessly and unselfishly as I could.

Whether or not I should have moved back to Lake Ann years earlier, I didn't know. What I did know in that moment as I headed to Lake Ann, was that I was going home; heart and soul. And I comfortably saw myself being there for the rest of my life.

I arrived in Lake Ann. It was well after dark, an

old platform rocker partly in, but mostly out, of the trunk.

The lights were on in the store, I drove to the front and looking in the windows could see the place full of people. I didn't even drive around back to park – just stopped in front of the store and got out. It was an unusually warm autumn night, the door was wide open and music poured out. I stepped in; quickly things got momentarily quiet. Dad walked over, shook my hand and said, "Welcome home, Son!" It was an interesting mix of people. I felt honored to be the evening's star attraction. There were long-time customers of the store who by nature of a small business such as ours, felt somehow attached to our family. There was Liz and some of her friends from work, the characters who comprised the town: Rich, Hazel, Pastor Brock, even Emma – Mom's friend who was with her when she died. Emma had a real hard time coming to terms with the tragedy. She tormented herself for days as she stubbornly viewed the situation as something that she should have been able to do something about – to prevent Mom's death.

On one occasion she called dad to see how he was doing. Somewhere along the line the conversation shifted to how she – Emma, was doing. Dad finally hearing enough declared, "Emma! I can't do this for you. I can barely keep a rational head about

Grace's death for myself. There isn't more of me left to help you! We could all prevent certain tragedies just by staying in bed! If you don't leave your house, you won't be in a traffic accident. But Grace and I didn't build a life together by being afraid of doing things, or speaking our minds. That's a kind of death of its own Emma. Maybe you should talk with the pastor or your doctor, Emma."

At any rate, it was good to see Emma out in public interacting with townsfolk and my family. Like Hazel, Emma was a widow, but more recently so. She had raised two sons, one lived on each coast. She saw them rarely, spoke with them seldom, but talked as though they all adored one another. I remember Mom and Dad talking about Emma, how she raised her sons to think each "was the center of the universe," implying that they – quite unlike our family – were of such greater importance as individuals than the family that they were a part of. Emma harped about the critical nature of building her son's self-esteems. Mom believed that there was a narrow path that separated self-esteem from self-centeredness and self-absorption. And that it was a mother's God-given right and duty to remind a child which side of that path they were on at any given time. "Mouthy brats probably killed Wallace," dad once spoke of the boys' father. "Probably just blew his cork from the inside."

Liz and I certainly weren't coddled by our parents.

I remember once, very young, wanting a new baseball. I wasn't allowed to have it, so I stole some money from the cash register. That was before I knew about cash register reconciliation at the end of the day. Also, dad took note of how I was consumed with interest with my new baseball. He confronted me. I lied. He took the baseball, put a screw in it and tied a string to it which he suspended high above the cash register. Neither of us spoke about it. Sometimes when I was in the store, someone would ask my dad about the baseball. He would simply say, "Ask Max." I responded by shrugging and saying, "I dunno." One day I finally admitted it was mine. It was there because I stole money from my mom and dad to get it. Dad wiped his hands and came from behind the counter, and standing between me and the customer who I was confessing to, asked me, "Anything else?"

"I lied about it," I said. At that moment, Dad reached up and yanked the string and baseball down. After the customer left, Dad went to the front door. He locked it, put up the closed sign and turned off the lights. As we walked through the back, he told Grandma and Grandpa we had "just closed early today." Then he called Mom at home and said; "Max and I are going to Elkton to the Ward's Store." He wanted to know if I wanted a new baseball, or a football. He told me I had learned my lesson about lying and stealing. I do not know if I understood that completely. But I did know that I would never again want to step outside of his powerful love for me.

I watched as Emma made her way over to Hazel. Together they were talking and laughing with Margo. There was an ease, a peace really to Margo's poise. It seemed like she had always been a part of us: our town, our business, my family, - me. I found myself moving, dodging people really, just to watch her. Now and then she appeared to scan faces for one in particular, so I approached her. She handed her drink to Emma – then she threw her arms around my neck, softly said, "Welcome home Max Bahle," and planted a kiss on my lips. Although I closed my eyes, I could somehow see in my mind Hazel's fleshy arms dancing about as she clapped and whelped in order to draw attention to Margo and me. That image quickly faded as I realized that it had been a long, long time since I was in the throes of an affectionate kiss. And maybe never had I sensed the fullness, and the warmth that comprised a kiss until that moment. She smiled as she pulled away. For the second time, it seemed like she blinked in slow motion. Was it her – or was it me – did she somehow alter my perception of time? Was I reacting in slow motion? I felt myself blink, but the only thought I had was that I sure hoped to be kissed like that again.

Throughout the evening as the crowd dwindled, it occurred to me that I had done the right thing. I couldn't imagine any way to derive more meaning from life than to be among those who I loved. Holding them in regard seemed to give life purpose. And to know that I was loved by them gave meaning to my thoughts and actions.

All was well in my world that autumn at Lake Ann.

Morning came quickly but there was not even a twinge of dread involving work. In fact I couldn't wait to be there. Dad would show up for awhile, and Saturday; the traditional market shopping day for many senior citizens would promise to be busy, if not unruly, with the likes of Hazel, the priest, the police chief and his wife stopping to pick up their orders. And of course Margo would be there.

I arrived early and put on coffee. The bakery had delivered baked goods which we sold retail. Most were pies that were special orders people would pick up during the day. The bakery closed at noon on Saturdays and we stayed open until 3:00 p.m. Most folks had learned over time to order from us if they didn't want to go to the bakery in the morning, or didn't want that additional errand, even though it was only a couple of miles out of town. Dad and Mom had enjoyed a successful business by offering service. People could simply call in their orders for meat, deli items and pies. We even cooked roasts, ribs; smoked chickens for customers to pick up. Of course we served food as well. Deli sandwiches to order, salads from the deli, a variety of coffees and teas and old fashioned sodas. Usually there were two soups served every day. Some was served to patrons who ate in the store, but most soup was sold for carry-out.

The market sold snacks and chips; marinade and seasonings, potatoes, lettuce – not too much produce really; and just bare bones groceries. People shopped for canned goods and dry goods in all their variety in Elkton. I would do the same the next day. After moving into my apartment it was necessary to stock-up on paper goods, laundry supplies, and hopefully some fresh fruit.

"Morning Max Bahle!" Margo's voice lilted as she strode in. Her face beamed in the morning as easily as any time of the day. She didn't wear make-up, and didn't need any. She just appeared robust and rosy and seemed genuinely cheery; all the time! She always seemed cheery. And it was infectious. People would come to the store pre-occupied, or a little too intent and serious about the perfect sirloin; then they would look at Margo's face, look into her eyes and somehow be changed. Maybe they just remembered that not every store, every clerk, every purchase had to be some kind of intense experience. We were there hour by hour to wait on our patrons; one at a time; intent on pleasing them. Sometimes that was accomplished by giving them exactly what they wanted, or by suggesting something else. In some instances patrons just needed some chit-chat amply dished up by any of the lively staff. Dad always thought of his work as a theatrical production. Sometimes he even would declare, "Showtime!" or "Curtain time!" over his shoulder as he opened the front door in the morning. I hoped that I would be capable of carrying on his tradition of service, his passion for it really.

One thing was certain to me; although many of my careerist contemporaries would disagree: It is enough in life, concerning work, to derive satisfaction from what it is you do. Formerly, although I could pat myself on the back for reducing the percentage of labor cost in manufactured goods, or achieving calendar quarters with no late or partial shipments, these seemed intangible somehow.

I was beginning to realize that life has meaning when people connect - eye to eye. It is undoubtedly low-tech, but sort of sensuous when you grab a big hunk of raw meat, hold it out in front of you and say, "Now that's a fine porterhouse Mr. Jones, how's it suit you?" There I would stand holding what would soon be that person's food. If you consider it biologically, food fuels the body to nourish, replenish and to some degree regenerate itself; there I was holding something physical that would in part become Mr. Jones. I had earlier cut that steak, then packaged it for him. I considered that to some degree I would participate in his meal. Maybe it was to celebrate some accomplishment. Maybe he just had a taste for this king of steaks that day. I wondered if he would eat all alone or if someone would be joining him. Or maybe he was feeding the children hot dogs. I hoped that he would eat in peace, and be satisfied. My work was beginning to mean something to me, and I realized what a pleasant reward that could be.

"Hey you! Deep in thought guy," Margo chided. "Wanna go fruit shopping at the supermarket in Elkton tomorrow?"

"Yeah, I was planning on it."

"Well, may I go along please?" She playfully pleaded.

"After church?" I questioned.

"Well, maybe instead of. Produce shopping is kind of spiritual." She rolled her eyes with the admission that her statement was at best quite a stretch in rationalization. In retrospect, I had to admit that produce shopping with Margo was sort of a spiritual experience. Maybe it was because I was so totally taken by her, it was easy to intently observe her, to really be absorbed in her energy and radiance, but in all honesty I don't think I ever watched anyone, so enjoy the process of picking their food, until that is I went with Margo.

She arrived at my apartment just before 8 o'clock Sunday morning. Her hair was down, and it was very long. As she walked towards the driver's door she began, "I thought I'd drive so you don't have to fret about shutting my hair in the car door."

I leaned over the top of the car facing her. "You don't miss much do you?" I asked referring to that night at dad's when Liz started to recount some of my teen-age dating disasters.

"Oh, I think it is so cute; there you were trying to be chivalrous and kind. Imagine the chance really, that the wind would blow her hair just as you shut the door. No harm done – just to your teenage pride. And the two of you were faced with an incident that helped you learn how to comfortably move beyond one of those awkward moments that dating couples have."

I moved back, bent over a bit, and pretended to open the door into my face. I staggered back a step, cupping both palms to my nose.

She seemed truly amused. She would have to learn that such reinforcement only encouraged me.

When she started the car, music began to play. It was a track from the Crosby, Stills and Nash album CSN. "My favorite group." I said, relaxing into my seat.

"Then or now?" Margo asked.

"Both."

"Me too." she said, sort of quietly, looking kind of serious and straight ahead as she drove.

Quickly the seriousness in her face faded and Margo appeared her charming, glowing self. I turned a bit towards her in my seat, although neither of us spoke. I enjoyed the drive. The autumn colors were beautiful with blazing crimson and orange maple trees, the brilliant golds and yellows of beech and hickory. There were still pockets of green, but mostly the vibrant hues of those magical weeks of fall.

"Hey, it's okay if we have the same favorite music group, isn't it?" I toyed.

Looking away from the road an instant, her face again momentarily serious; "I just keep getting 'weirded out' by you Max. I mean that was us way back then with the sno-cones on your bike. I used to cry about that sometimes, how I should have told those girls that I liked grape flavored sno-cones too, and should have chose you over them. I dreamed about you, about riding on your bike, the wind in my hair. I'd see us riding past that bait store where they sold all that candy….."

"I know where all those girls live, wanna go beat'em up?" I mused.

Margo chuckled but wiped one of her moist eyes, "I am just really, really feeling like I came back here just to meet you Max."

"Basically, I'm a chick magnet. A real smooth, cool, operator. Remember when I met you? You thought I was stealing a sandwich. My heart was in my throat, Margo. You did that to me. That's a chemical thing – or a gland thing or something isn't it? Did my mom track you down? Is this some kind of plot? My family likes you more than they like me – don't you think that you are kind of 'weirding out' my life too?" I was in rare form.

"You…" she said smiling and shaking her head. She dropped her right hand from the steering wheel; my left hand met it on the seat beside her thigh.

After coffee and a donut from a quaint little donut shop on the outskirts of Elkton, we arrived at the supermarket. I overly dramatized wrestling a shopping cart from the line of cart clones, hoping the one I chose wasn't a mutant one with a skidding or wobbling wheel. Amidst my clanging and jerking I defiantly announced, "And this is why we don't have these damned shopping carts at Bahle's!"

An amused Margo played along, "But you managed to wrestle one free for little ol' me?" She plunked her purse down in the cart and put her arm around my back sliding her thumb between my jeans and shirt and lightly grasping my belt. It felt good.

Natural. The added weight of her arm made me sense my pants slip down a bit. I had always had trouble keeping pants in place. Dad did too. Liz used to call us the "butt crack brothers." Mom however was more tender: "Poor boys just don't have enough butt to keep their drawers in place," she would say.

"Um, I hope you're not planning on yanking my pants down here in the store," I sternly cautioned: "I'm not wearing clean underwear."

Margo squeezed me hard and rolled her head into my shoulder. "Max you just spoil all my fun."

She left me for the mangos. I stood with the cart, out of the main aisle, but with my gaze fixed on her. She picked up a fruit, cupped it in both hands and felt it. Her eyes closed. She smelled it, like she was inhaling aromatherapy or something. She sat it aside. A keeper I suspected. I watched as she shifted her weight to one leg and leaned her hip casually and comfortably into the front of the produce case as she meticulously selected her fruit. She motioned to me to retrieve a bag from her containing her choice selections. She quickly kissed my cheek or my neck each time as we moved to pears, then on to tomatoes, then kiwis.

This ritual seemed reverent, solemn; important. It did seem like a spiritual experience. A kind of substitute for the liturgy I was missing. A woman so sensitive, so concerned about her fresh fruit, would surely have to be good to me I thought. My head jolted, responding to how silly that thought seemed. You're falling in love with each other, just leave it at that I thought to myself. And it had been so long, it seemed like I had to learn how all over again. But that would be okay, because choosing to love; building and maintaining it, nurturing it really into something mutually beneficial and mutually fulfilling is the greatest of human endeavors.

There I was at the supermarket, in the produce section with this angel-like woman in blue jeans and a corduroy shirt. Right then I felt as though there was nowhere else I'd rather be, nothing else I'd rather be doing. Because of her everything was, in that moment, perfect. Isn't it a wonder when you love like that?

We moved along, got my 16 rolls of paper towels, 48 rolls of toilet paper. "Forty-eight Max? Forty-eight rolls of toilet paper?" Margo kept querying as though she might cause my rational mind to spring open and evaluate my quirky need to never fall below 24 rolls, ever. "You mean there are always 24 in a cabinet or closet or something?" She seemed to be astonished.

"Yep. Except for one time I remember getting the flu real bad. Might have ended up with only 22, or 23."

"Must've been horrible for you." Her arm draped

over my shoulders.

"Let me tell ya! Sick, and stressed; I'm sure it impeded my recovery." I spoke humorously about it, even though it still really felt reasonable for a single, healthy person to have so much toilet paper.

"Well, check out Liz sometime." I needed to shift from the subject of my mildly neurotic notion to someone else whom I knew and considered to be worse off than me. "She has inventories." I continued, "So much flour, so much sugar in the downstairs freezer. So many bottles of mustard, catsup, peanut butter – you name it. When we were little we took playing store very seriously. It was really in our blood you know. Just never outgrew it I guess."

"So, you've got a thing – what is it? Everybody's got a thing." I shifted to Margo.

"Nope. Clean." She pursed her lips and shook her head not defensive at all, just self-assured.

I pointed my finger at her and bent it slightly like it was old and gnarled and announced in my best wicked witch of the west voice, "I'll get you my pretty! I'll find your neurotic thing!"

We stuffed our purchases into Margo's car and headed back to Lake Ann. Slowly she drove past the store and my apartment. "Um, are we taking the scenic route or are you just kidnapping me?" I asked.

"Maybe it's time I show you my place."

"Oh, I see you think I'm sleazy, cheap and easy.

Just take me up to your den of iniquity. Have your way with me, just to get to my family's enormous wealth and power!" I teased. She laughed, but we were both a bit uncomfortable. Thank goodness there were groceries to carry.

Margo's house was not only beautiful, but evoked a sense of calm from me. Mostly arts and crafts style furnishings and decorating; it made sense in relation to her personality. Straight lines and symmetry bespoke of her straightforwardness and the unflinching consistency of her character strengths.

We looked at pictures and relics and artifacts from her parental legacy. "That's all I have to offer you Max. I'm so sorry I can't introduce you to my mom, or my dad." Her eyes watered. "Your mom made me feel like it was okay for me to be here. Like she would make sure that I was part of something intimate: the store, her family, the community, something, I don't know what. I need to be part of something, of someone. I want it to be you Max. Are you the one I've been searching for?" I wrapped my arms around her.

"I sure hope so," I whispered.

My eyes were drawn to a picture and an object nearly hidden by it on a small table, a few feet away. I discontinued our embrace and moved towards it, "Your mom?" I asked.

"Yeah." Behind the picture was an open pack of cigarettes in a sealed case, the kind you would use to keep a treasured baseball for instance.

"Maybe I just found your 'thing.' That idiosyn-cratic, or neurotic notion that I was trying to com-pare to my toilet paper 'thing'."

"I smoked in college. Well, for that matter when I started my career – but usually at night at clubs or bars with friends and co-workers. The accounting firm I worked for in Indianapolis was one of the early converts to smoke-free offices."

"So you were a good team player and gave it up?" I asked.

"Well, yes I gave it up, but it didn't have any-thing to do with work. I enjoyed smoking – the ritual. The process really; from taking it out of the pack, getting it lit, sitting back, inhaling then exhaling that first puff. It was my mother – that's why I quit. She smoked forever it seemed. At one time smoking seemed sort of classy. Mom hung on to that kind of identity. That pack of cigarettes was in my purse when Mom called and said she had emphysema, and it was caused by smoking. I just put that pack in a drawer that evening. A few years later, after she died of lung cancer, I bought the display case. It repre-sents to me the cost of smoking, sitting there beside Mom's picture."

While her words indicated her strength of con-viction, she didn't seem bitter or remorseful. It was just a matter of fact.

"I'm sorry Margo." I was. And I didn't really know what else to say. "You have had significant losses Margo."

"But I couldn't change the circumstances so I can't be controlled by them. I can't hold on to bitterness, or sadness. It really isn't very complicated when you realize that some things in life simply are as they are. We can choose to triumph, or not. And then we all have to find our own way of getting through these things."

"Have there been other things you have given up?" I asked.

Ready to change the subject Margo said, "Yes. During Lent once, I gave up worrying. Instead of worring, I'd have a drink to calm my anxiousness. It didn't work out so well. By Easter I was practically a drunk."

"Max, are you a little hungry?" Margo pulled a covered plate out of the refrigerator. It had slices of ring bologna, sliced dill pickles and chunks of raw sweet onion. She un-wrapped the plate then put it on a serving tray, took a box of crackers out of the cupboard and told me to get a couple sodas out of the refrigerator.

"This is just about the greatest snacking in the world – I can't believe it! You eat like this too?" I was just shocked with yet another coincidence of our commonality.

"No." She spoke flatly then smiling in a mocking sort of way and batting her eyelids said, "Your daddy told me." She walked away and instructed me to "come." Obediently, I followed. She sat the tray on a small table in front of a wicker couch in the sunroom. We sat down, I was on one end. She grabbed a piece of onion, a slice of pickle and bologna, assembled it in a stack and asked, "Just like this?"

"Cracker is optional," I reassured her.

"Not bad," she mumbled. As quick and agile as a cat threw her legs up on the couch and reclined resting her head in my lap. She rolled forward a bit and pointed at the lake, beautifully visible in a panoramic view, "This is why I wanted this house. I pictured myself just sitting or laying here and silently passing the hours gazing out." She patted my knee, "Now you're here. I think things are really improving." She exhaled a comfortable, relaxing sigh.

"So should I eat onion or not?" I asked innocently and serious, attempting to be considerate in the event that the day may hold the promise of some kissing.

"Is it something I may need to get used to?" She rolled her head a bit, looking me in the face although sideways and upside down. She was biting the corner of her lower lip as comfortable as if we had sat like this for years.

"Probably." I put the snack in my mouth that I had been holding since I sat down. I beamed one of those smiles that felt like my mouth would burst open in laughter – as I chewed.

Sensing my subdued laugh, she covered her face with her hands and speaking through laughter asked, "This isn't going to turn into one of those awkward moments is it?" She drew one of her knees towards her chest.

I swallowed hard, "No," I spoke, "thankfully."

She dramatically relaxed her pose with a, "Whew!"

"So how's it feel, moving back home and working with your dad, in what is now a third generation family business?" Margo probed.

"It feels really good. I can't even imagine why I didn't do this before now. I hadn't liked my job especially, didn't really like living in Greenfield. I guess I had just come to be comfortable with a certain sameness. After my teaching career got flushed down the toilet and Alice died – I think I just tried to hide away. Next thing I know, 15 years went by. The day Liz called about Mom sure has set into motion an interesting chain of events. But I'm having a problem at work. Might have to bring it up to Dad one of these days."

"Your back hurts or something?" Margo was intent and serious.

"No. I've got a problem with one of the other

workers."

"You do?" She seemed surprised, given my laid back manner.

"Yeah, she kind of paws and gropes me a lot." Margo reached up and twisted my ear, but didn't say anything. I sensed that she had a more serious agenda. She did "Were you ever in love after Alice?"

"No." "Well except for now maybe."

She held two fingers together, kissed them and pressed them to my lips, then, "Did you date many people?"

"Three. Not at first, of course. But I chased the first one off eventually because I hadn't really come to terms with grief."

"Took a long time to get over Alice's death?" Margo asked.

"Well, not just her. But yes it did. Maybe it sounds odd, but I think I grieved the loss of my job as well. After all, there is hope and expectation built into a career, especially after training for it, spending the time, energy and money for the education, espousing all of my ideals and goals. And I didn't have a plan B. I was devastated. I truly believe I grieved that as well as Alice's death. Finally, while I was reading something once, it occurred to me that I had become cynical – almost bitter, and I realized that I couldn't be happy and so cynical at the same time. I sensed that it was teaching that I hadn't gotten over. Liz had an experience that hit her hard as a veterinarian and she beat that demon by altering her career and life direction."

"Yes, she's told me about that." Margo responded.

"Well, she advised me to pitch out my teaching stuff. So I got together lesson plans I had kept, papers, handouts and guidelines for methods, resources – everything; just everything. I put it in boxes, and late one Sunday night, took it to the curb for the garbage man."

"Good for you!" Margo slapped my knee.

"There's more. I sat in a lawn chair with twelve of Dad's homebrews. I'd wake up, run up to the apartment to pee, then, go back, drink myself to sleep and wait for the garbage man. I didn't wake up until he was in front of the house, believe me, those trucks are noisier when you are up close and personal. He looked at me as he picked up my stuff and threw it into the truck. I handed him the remaining unopened beers and shook his hand and told him thanks. Then I folded up my chair and went into the house."

"You Bahle's are a strange bunch of people." Margo rolled her head and looked me in the eye. She blinked. Again it seemed like I watched her eyes in slow motion, like we were in some kind of time warp. "Well what about two; and three?" She asked.

"Well a few years went by between one and two.

Two, as you call her, was a divorcee with two small children, a combative and jealous ex-husband, and she needed care and support; not a boyfriend or lover. Three, as we shall call her, came a few months later, she loved malls, clothes, cosmetics and her physical self. While I read the newspaper she laid out clothes on the bed in varying combinations to pre-plan attire for the next few days. However, this planning was interrupted by weather, what someone else wore, if she bloated… She was uninteresting, unable to connect emotionally; and yet for months I desperately clung to her. Once, I was home, here, for a weekend by myself and mom told me to "go inside myself." She told me to be contemplative, meditative, and begin reading to engage my mind again. Her advice was good. I came to terms with being a bachelor. Everything was fine until 'four' came along."

"Would that be me?" Margo asked.
"Uh-huh."

CHAPTER 4
FINDING OUR WAY HOME

"You would have been a great teacher, Max."

"Thanks. The kids who would fall through the cracks, the marginal students – they responded to me. The first day of school, I'll never forget it. It was a good memory. Not a glory day that I hang on to like someone who hasn't had any successes since then, but just a magical episode of connecting to a handful of kids. I told them I didn't care what any of them did last year, I wasn't there. And I, like them, would be starting with a clean slate. I told them I was hired with the expectation that I'd be an excellent teacher – unless I proved otherwise. That was sort of an ironic if not prophetic thing to say wasn't it, Margo?" I asked rhetorically. "Anyway, I told the students that I had the same idea about them. I announced that everyone had standards and expectations to meet. I had these items on the chalkboard, and had them on a handout which spelled out how well they needed to score on quizzes, tests, projects, all that crap. Then I said, you all begin with an A. It's up to you if you keep it or settle for less. Most of the kids went nuts – they whooped and hollered a minute or two. The brightest students looked like I'd socked them in the gut as they looked at each other, and blankly at me. That's how the assistant principal and principal responded too, by the way. But it went well. I spoke to every pupil during each grading period about their performance and we talked about the grade they were heading for. They were making choices and most thought they were in control of their grades, at least within the guidelines and structure that I imposed on them. But who knows if it made a difference or not. Ancient history."

"So any regrets, unfinished business, dragons to slay…" Margo was drawing her questions to a close. I let my head drop backwards. I seriously pondered but couldn't think of anything as I surveyed the ceiling. I realized how comfortable and relaxed I felt, I was running my hand partway along her thigh and hip. Her warmth made me feel cozy. There was a calm fullness in my chest. Where there had been a void, now I felt completeness; almost otherworldly, euphoric, even a bit giddy perhaps.

"Yes." It came to me. I always wanted to follow the plains harvest. And I want a '58 Willy's pick-up truck."

"OK, wait…" Margo began. "I know what a

truck is although I don't know about a '58 Willy's. But what's the plains harvest? Like grain harvest?"

"Yeah! Yeah. It starts in maybe Texas, depending on the company and their crews then they just move up the country, some even into Canada. Just harvesting wheat until there is no more!"

"And this is something you still want to do," Margo seemed concerned.

"No, no. Oh, God no. It's a bitch of a job. It's for people half my age. But, it's regret. I should've done it. Not a big emotionally draining regret, more of a curiosity really. The Willy's, that's unfinished business. I'm going to own one; really. Is it my turn to play 20 questions yet?" I queried.

"Fair enough Max Bahle."

"So let's switch."

She got up. "OK, see I sit down where you are at. And you lay your head in my lap."

"What will you do if I don't ever want to get up and leave?"

"I'll take that chance," she smiled.

"Do you have some wine or beer or something?" I was eating more bologna and pickle. Leaving the onion really seemed the right thing to do at this stage of our relationship.

"Oh, no!" "I don't have any wine, Max. I meant to get some, but just haven't. I have some beer your dad gave me. I have to tell you, I think it's strong. I just don't have a taste for it. But could I get you one?"

"No."

"Um…." She was embarrassed.

"Hey. How about a glass of water?" I asked.

"With lime?" she asked as she walked back into the kitchen.

"Sure! Teach me a little class, would ya!" I hoped to make her feel better. We hadn't quite finished our sodas, but they were warm. I took them to the kitchen. Margo plinked some ice in two tumblers and took cut slices of lime from a container on the counter.

"I always have some lime or lemon in water. Sometimes even a squirt of cider vinegar. Gives it a little taste, makes it interesting. Is all of this, ok? My questioning, that is?" she asked.

"Let's go back to the magic room." I gestured toward the path we had just trod. The sunroom was bright and warm. The view outside was stunning with the sun overhead causing the water to glisten. I allowed her to sit down. Quickly she slapped her thighs. I hadn't lain on a couch with my head in someone's lap for twenty years. It felt awkward for an instant. I felt like I would squish her.

Sensing my awkwardness, she cupped her hand over my ear and pushed down on my head, "Max, I know you've got a lot of brains in your head, but it's really not that heavy. You won't break me."

"Maybe you're afraid I'll pull a dry cleaning bag from behind the couch and mercilessly suffocate you, as I've done to so many others before you." She slid her hand between her thigh and my cheek when I didn't laugh or react and held it to my cheek as I turned my head to see her face, her eyes.

"Margo, you asked if it was okay for you to ask, to know about my life. I will be with you as we sit in silence or if you want to watch TV. I will talk with you for hours if you can stand it, if you find me interesting. That's how it will be with me. I read, listen to certain radio programs, sometime I listen to music, sometimes I watch TV. I want to visit with my dad and sister. Hazel. And if you would go along, maybe even get into a card game at the Clubhouse sometime. My mind is curious, but not restless. I don't need a lot of diversions. I like to be home. If you choose to love me, you must know that I am re-energized by the solace of home and believe in home as refuge. I will not leave you for hunting trips, routine boy's nights out, I don't care about a speedboat, snowmobile, motorcycle, camping trailer, big screen TV. I like pontoon boat rides in the morning and at evening. I don't take up much space, just a few books, clean socks, and if you let me lay in your lap for the rest of your life, I promise to be your faithful companion."

Her tears dripped on my face and she alternately

choked laughter and sobs, "What a good puppy Max, someday I just may ask your daddy if I can bring you home."

I wiped her tears away as her smile beamed. "But I am going to trade my car for a '58 Willy's truck. By the way, I'll tell Dad you don't care for his beer-"

Margo interrupted, "Oh, no Max! Please don't!"

Sorry to alarm her, I touched her cheek. "It's okay Pumpkin – see, he will get to work brewing something you like. Like Belgian lambics. Malts infused with cherries; called krieks, or raspberry, or pineapple. He will find something you like. It'll be good for him. Give him something to do."

She just looked at me. I began to consider how ironic that just as Dad was learning to live alone after all those years with Mom, I was learning to love this woman holding my head, learning to be with someone after years of being alone. I didn't pity Dad, because he seemed to be okay. From my own experience, I believed a person could live alone or coupled so long as it resolved into intent, and there was purpose and peace. I hoped for peace for my Dad, and that as he shifted his perceived life's purpose, I hoped that it would continue to have meaning for him, and he could find fulfillment.

"You called me Pumpkin."

"I'm sorry Margo, I didn't mean any disrespect, it just kind of slipped out-" I started to raise myself up; she pushed me down and patted me. "- Mom and Dad called Liz and I Pumpkin. I don't even know why I – it's not part of my routine vocabulary-"

"I like it. I haven't heard anyone called that in thirty years. I think my dad maybe called me that." Her eyes watered.

"I sure am making you cry a lot." I apologized. Margo was sentimental, and sweet, and sensitive. But intelligent: and savvy too.

She cleared her throat and took some water. "My dad died when I was almost 13. That summer, on your bike; it was that following autumn he died. Mom and I never came back here. I did in my mind. But it must've been upsetting to her and I never asked. After she died, I came up for a weekend a couple of times. Now here I am. Because of the life insurance, Mom was suddenly wealthy. We left Kokomo, and moved to Indianapolis. I went to a private school. She got a real estate license and dabbled, but mostly liked the social aspect, being connected. But she began to buy apartments. I went to Butler, became an accountant, was hired by the firm where Mom was a client and had a career for a decade or so. Finally, she suggested I open a small office in one of our buildings, if I wanted to. So, for another – almost decade – I worked part-time primarily as Mom's bookkeeper. I dealt with superintendents of buildings, rental managers and lenders.

I know it sounds spoiled and pampered, but I just didn't like it. As she got sicker, I cared for her. We began to get out of properties and went into real estate investment trusts to avoid capital gains. When she died, I sold the rest of her real estate and took the tax consequences. She had some secrets though. Somehow there was a trust I didn't know anything about, and the matter of a one million dollar life insurance policy of which I was beneficiary."

"You don't exactly need to work at the store do you Margo?" I smiled.

"Not really. But I hope to for a long, long time." She smiled back.

"I was lucky to have both of my parents as long as I did. Being a butcher's son, I can tell you, we ate good. We always had the lake here to enjoy. We were held in regard in the community, and since it is a small town, I always felt safe and protected. My childhood was great. I'm just really sorry you grew up without your dad, Margo."

"Well, thank you Max. My mom overcompensated. She loved me – I'm convinced of that. But she pampered me. I wanted a lot from men because of her, I think. I probably overlooked some decent, good guys because I demanded they be men of means. And because Dad wasn't there, I think I wanted a father's approval and affection. While I was with the accounting firm I sort of cozied up to businessmen and lawyers. Each one I became involved with was much older than me. One was actually old enough to have been my father. What I thought was power and self-assurance, really amounted to arrogance and self-absorption. All of them had ruined marriages, some multiple times. The last one gave me a ring but couldn't commit to a wedding date. He dangled me along over a year before finally taking me to a concert and telling me that it just wasn't prudent for him to divorce his wife. So I spent a couple of years being a touch-me-not, raving, man hating bitch. I was warmly welcomed into the angry wives and divorcees club. Talk about cynicism; I had a stretch of time like that, too. I knew I was unhappy, but didn't know how to become happy. Quite accidentally, Mom and I together, bought this old farm house. I moved into it myself. I threw myself into creating a place where I would want to come home to. I started flower beds and gardens. Went to some adult education classes and began to be comfortable with myself and my new found green thumb. When winter came I decided to learn sourdough bread baking. I read some of the pop psycho-babble popular at the time. The next year I took a food preserving course through the extension agency. I learned to can corn and freeze peaches. I got a farmer's tan because of my sleeveless T-shirts and cut-offs. I had stopped wearing make-up. I hadn't

planned to, but only working part-time, and princi-
pally for myself – well, Mom really; I would drive
into the city in jeans and flannel shirts. And eventually came to realize that whenever I left home, I left
my heart there. Mom didn't know what to make of
it, really, but was at that time becoming mostly concerned about herself; her health that is. That was three
or four years ago. I had hired this old, Dutch guy to
wallpaper my kitchen. He worked slowly. He freely
told me everything I needed to know about paper-
ing. He even brought rolls of different kinds of paper throughout the week to have me paste and hang
just to see how they felt different. I didn't know if
we would ever get the kitchen finished, but I think I
could do it to suit myself. I invited him for lunch at
some point, and so we began to eat together and talk.
I just opened up to him like he was my grandpa."

"So you dated this old Dutch guy?" I couldn't
resist a perfect opportunity for sarcasm.

Consistently capable of beating me at this game
of wit she replied, "Yes and we together had grey-
haired babies who have moved back to the Nether-
lands."

"I thought you said this was three or four years
ago." I volleyed.

She pressed a finger to my lips, "Let me finish
Mr. Smarty Pants. He told me I had one obligation:
To honor and care for my mother as best I could. He

said my heart would guide me if I listened. He told me to choose a man whose eyes neither stared nor shifted. Honesty and flexibility could be found in a man's eyes, he said. He told me to hold a man's hands, to watch how he moved his hands. Men with pride and passion moved their hands slowly, deliberately. And regarding warmth, as are the hands, so is the heart. His last day there he put his strong warm hand to the back of my neck and kissed my forehead. He said a lovely but chilling thing: 'He who you seek waits for you. He waits in a place where you also want to be.' I wrote down what he said. It's in my purse. Then he said: "After supper, here, by yourself, clean your dishes, then turn down the lights and sit back down at the table. Close your eyes and keep repeating to yourself, say out loud, but slowly these words: 'Be still.' If it makes you feel good, do it the next night, and so on."

"So did you?" I asked.

"Yep. And moved in with Mom. When it became evident she wouldn't get better, I sold my house. We had health care come into her house and I did everything I could. She got tired of being in and out of the hospital. And finally came home to die. I stayed in her house not quite two years after she died. Then I came to this place where I wanted to be. And here you are."

She sat there running the backs of her fingernails over my forehead and through my hair, not saying a word. Suddenly she blurted out, "The end."

"Wait, wait!" I said and sat up. "Did they live happily ever after?"

"Yes! Oh, yes!" She exclaimed.

And next, I was glad I hadn't eaten any more onion.

"I should probably be going home, if you would be so kind," I suggested. "I've been going over to Dad and Liz's house on Sunday afternoons, and they may be expecting me."

"As you wish, but what would you say to the idea of inviting them here, Max?"

"Hey, that's a great idea as far as I'm concerned. I'm not sure I can speak for Dad. Liz wouldn't object I don't imagine."

"Well give them a ring." Margo handed me a cordless phone.

"Hi Pop. Would you and Liz be up for a slight change of routine?" I asked.

"Maybe." he replied, "What have you got in mind?"

"Well, maybe you and Liz could come over here." Margo was intently watching and listening to me. Noting that I hadn't said, "her house," she was pointing to the floor with darting motions and mouthing the word, "here." It occurred to me that Dad probably thought I meant my apartment. I clarified, "I mean here at Margo's. I'm at Margo's house."

"You're at Margo's? What the hell are you doing there?" I suppose it was a natural response,
maybe a surprise, but because of the confusion by
my choice of words, I think he was puzzled for a
second or two. Then I heard him laughing as I put
the phone to my chest. It was an odd moment, a defining one. It hadn't been unusual to mention to Dad,
Liz, well anyone really, that I intended to get to know
Margo better. But after the previous hours we had
spent together talking and holding one another, I
thought that things were suddenly very different for
Margo and me. We would no longer be casual. I
hadn't fully processed this in my own mind, I wasn't
sure that I wanted to start explaining it to Dad. I
held the phone close to my body to mute my words.
I spoke to Margo: "He wants to know what I'm doing here."

She giggled. "Well, I took you to the store, you
carried in my groceries."

"She took me to the supermarket, Dad. Then I
carried in her groceries."

"Something wrong with your car, Max?" He
seemed concerned. "You should've called."

"Potato and ham soup didn't sell out yesterday;
I thought we'd have that. Want me to bring it?" He
asked. "Hey, does she play cards, Max?"

"Just a second Dad." I held my hand over the

phone and asked Margo: "Ham and potato soup? Got two decks of cards?" She nodded yes. "Fine, Dad. Got it covered. Come about 5:30 or 6 o'clock?"

"Ok, Son. Liz is working. I'll wait on her to get home. Might be more like 6:30."

We sprang into action. To my delight there was more bologna, pickles and onion. Not only had I been preoccupied with Margo earlier, but also wanted to make a good impression. Living alone, I could turn a snack or hors d'oeuvres into a meal.

Sensing I was with a civilized woman, I tried to mind my manners. At any rate, Dad and Liz would certainly like those leftovers. Margo knelt down and pulled a bag from the cupboard. Oyster crackers for the soup. Dad was just going to love this woman.

Margo placed soup bowls on pretty plates and handed them to me to set on the table. I placed the bowl near the edge of the table at each place setting, with the plate behind each bowl. She stopped what she was doing and walked towards me. She put both hands on her hips, looked long at the table, then me. She seemed perplexed.

"Was I supposed to keep the bowl on the plate?" I asked innocently. I went on: "Margo, we Bahle's are a mongrel hoard. We are frontier folk who have been in this country since the early 1700's. Forgive us: we know not what we do."

She smiled and picked up the plates. She stacked

them on the counter; then turned around to face me. She leaned back against the edge of the countertop and grasped it with both hands. I stood at the table and faced her.

"This is the first of a thousand things," I told her, "-that one of us will feel alien to, or dislike. I hope, Margo, to have what Mom and Dad had. Go to work and be together, go home and be together. Neither one needed to say, 'I love you,' but they did. Dad always used cream in his coffee, but Mom always asked. I don't know why she did. I don't know why he didn't say, "For God's sake woman I've used cream in my coffee for over 50 years!" But he never did. This is going to seem kind of weird for awhile, I'm afraid. But I will be honest and forthright and gentle with you. If something is a big deal, I'll try to tell you why. If something else is a pet peeve, I'll try to explain why. I'm up for the challenge because I may learn that I have ideas or attitudes without basis. Being a couple can make us better as individuals too, don't you think?"

"I can't say that I have ever had a companion who aspired to be a better person because we were together," Margo began, "Never have I known a man who acknowledged at this early stage in our relationship that effort was involved, and candid discussions about differences of opinion would be welcomed and even necessary. Actually, approaching a relationship this way is probably easier than the typical pattern of attempting to ignore a lot of little things; until stacked one on top of the other, one single thing finally causes all the others to cascade down in anger, frustration or hurt. I think your folks established their life in peace. That's what I want. I want to live in peace. With you; Max."

The doorbell rang. I walked with Margo to answer it. The priest and Dad were standing there.

"Welcome gentlemen," Margo greeted them, then nodding to the priest spoke, "Father," then nodding with her head tilting toward a shoulder and winking at Dad, said "Father." Dad put her hand into both of his and smiled at her.

"Where's Liz?" she asked.

"Oh, she'll be along. I invited the Father along. There's plenty of soup. Says he has something to show our family. And he has a jug of wine."

Dad and the priest were given a tour of her home by Margo. I brought the wine and soup into the house and put the soup on the stove, set an extra bowl for the priest, then decided to put plates under the bowls. Margo came back into the kitchen about that time and seeing what I was doing, strolled over and kissed me on the cheek.

"Maybe we should cut up some of that fruit we bought this morning," she suggested.

"Any special way – or something you have in mind?" I asked.

Her reply was simple, "Surprise me."

Believe it or not, I actually knew how to halve an apple, cut segments of it and shirr them back to resemble the layers of feathers a swan has. Then I cut a segment that would become the neck and head once affixed with a toothpick. Next I sliced kiwi and placed around my swan. They looked like giant mutant lily pads I thought. Finally, I whacked up some mango and attempted to arrange it before finally just sort of pitching it all over. Good or bad, I was pretty certain that my fruit platter would be a surprise to Margo. *"Only one way to find these things out."* I thought to myself.

Liz arrived and we all sat at the table and had our supper.

"Who carved the apple swan, or goose, or whatever?" Dad wanted to know. "Very creative," noted the priest.

"Isn't it cute?" beamed Margo. "Swimming around there among the lily pads..." "Oh, God, you've gone goo-goo." Liz looked at her and began to laugh.

"Is there a budding romance here?" The old priest innocently inquired.

Without any consideration, I simply blurted out; "I love Margo."

After a moment of silence, Liz leaned back in her chair, comfortable, if not intoxicated with the opportunity to make me squirm a little. "Well, we all love Margo. She's a wonderful person, Max."

I leaned over my bowl towards my sister. I was actually glad that she was putting me in a situation to articulate a thought based on my mounting feelings: "Yes, but I'm in-love with Margo." I leaned back into my chair sort of cocky. Sort of "Liz-style." I heard Margo gasp – "Oh Max!" And she scooted her chair close to mine.

"Really?" Dad looked at us. "Very fine!"

"May I propose a toast to the fine young couple?" The old priest raised his glass without waiting for any response.

As Liz raised her glass she leaned over her bowl, her eyes danced from Margo to me. There was no sarcasm in her face and she softly said, "Good for you. Both of you."

"I guess the night is full of surprises Father," Dad offered.

"Shall I show them now?" He asked Dad, then got up to get a small package he had left with his coat.

"I sure wish Grace were here. I wish she could have known about this, kids." Dad spoke to Margo and me.

"I think she was the first to know Will," Margo suggested to him.

"Weeks ago, I sent a letter to Erik Von Rath's

old address. I wrote 'Bakery' since I did not know the names of the young couple who had bought the bakery. I sent a clipping from the newspaper and the obituary of Grace, and the death announcement of Erik. They called me. They were sorry they hadn't tried to contact him because they had found this packet of photos. I suspect these were of him, his parents, possibly some customers. The couple suggested that perhaps the church could donate money which they receive from Erik's estate to the town for a guardrail along the lake; then dedicate it with a memorial to him and Grace. Attorneys for the diocese are still working on the estate of course, but by next summer we should know where we stand. What do you all think about this?"

"I told the Father it's great," Dad added. Liz, Margo and I all agreed.

We all continued to talk awhile. Then Dad, the old priest and Liz left. Margo wanted to know when she was to take me and my toilet paper home. As we drove back to my apartment in the darkness of the evening, the dash lights illuminated her face. This wonderful person, this beautiful woman was a gift from all the best that heaven and earth had to offer, to me.

"You caught me a bit off guard tonight at supper, Max." Margo broke our silence. "I'm sorry," I said.

"Well, don't be. I guess I just assumed that I would hear it said first – directly to me."

"I suppose you will always remember the first time you heard it then, won't you?" I laughed.

Margo helped me carry my groceries upstairs. She even helped me put things away – except for the toilet paper. She seemed pretty sure that something was wrong about wanting that much and she just couldn't be party to helping me stow it away. I was pretty sure she was kidding because the following weekend she invited me over just to peek into a closet where sixty rolls of my favorite brand of toilet paper, were shelved. "I wanted to make sure you felt safe here, Max." She toyingly spoke then smiled.

"Well, I guess this is the time when I'm supposed to say good night," Margo began as she moved toward me.

"We have had a lot of changes to our lives of late, Margo. And today we talked about some things that neither of us has had the chance to share with anybody else. I don't want to rush ahead to something that makes the impact of today less important. Will that be ok?" I asked as I held her tightly to me.

"Well that takes the pressure off," she sighed, "I love you Max Bahle."

"Well, I love you Margo Stephens. If you can't sleep, you call me," I said.

I wasn't at all sure that there was such a thing as

love at first sight. I acknowledge that when I was a boy, I was taken with Margo, while she too, was a child. Our first encounter as adults, at Dad's store was at once perplexing and powerfully wonderful. We were both young middle-aged people who through love, loss, and living had distilled a reasonable set of principles that functioned to give our lives purposeful meaning. We both had become weary of the search for a companion, and had learned to be comfortable with our individual selves. About 1:00 a.m. my telephone rang. I answered, hoping it was Margo. It was.

"Hello Max. I seemed to have found a roll of toilet paper in the car," she toyed, "I'm wondering if you have only 47 in your closet? What do you do in such situations?"

"I think you are getting way too much enjoyment with this ridicule," I replied.

"I suppose you're right. I'm not sleeping and I've slept pretty good ever since I moved here I'll have you know. I've got to ask, Max, it's the store isn't it? You wonder if I could keep an interest in it, don't you?" she asked.

"Listen sweet Margo, I came back to it, having worked there off and on over the course of my life. Now I find that it is what I want to do with the rest of my working life. My lifestyle is in synch with this retail, and seasonal business. Plus, I've made quite a commitment to my dad."

"I understand those choices and the way you feel about them, Max," Margo interjected. "Max, I am not running from something. I left friends and opportunity in Indianapolis. I came to Lake Ann because it seemed to give me soulful rest. The natural beauty: the quaintness; and my sense of history too. You may have grown up here, loving this place. Maybe not even knowing how much so until you left it. "This much I know, Max. My family loved the times we had here. I'm not leaving."

"I'll bet you think I haven't considered the permanent change to my lifestyle if I become a partner in your life and your business. I cannot speak from experience, but I try to imagine the lifestyle. No summer vacations. Ever. So I promise to make each sunset over the lake something to celebrate with you. Each summer we train kids to help. Each winter we work hard together to survive on only local trade. Before I met you Max, I fell in love with this cycle of seasons, this combination of business and living, because your mom talked about it with me. She spoke about her town, her family, her husband, with a gleam in her eye. I suspected that she had an insight, something I could learn about balancing all of those things and still having passion for them all."

"Wow!" I declared. "I'm so sorry that I didn't talk about this with you yet."

"By the way, Bub," she sarcastically began,

"short of those sandwiches you pilfer, the store is in a good cash position. I've asked a lot of questions of the vendors, and I have some suggestions, although I have been unsure how to approach you or your dad. Before you get the wrong impression, my concerns were that your dad might not be ready to hear suggestions for change so soon after your Mom's passing. Also, I confess that I didn't want to challenge or upstage you, especially since you are just getting reestablished with the business. Those concerns have just dissolved away today Max. I promise to disclose to you any such thoughts I have, and look forward to you and I learning to compromise, and learning to accept that at times one of us will doggedly persevere. And the other must learn to accept those decisions and realize that life and love are much bigger things."

After excitedly saying all that; she paused. I was silent.

"Max, are you there? You didn't fall asleep did you?" she asked.

"Not by any stretch of the imagination would that be possible," I replied. "This is important. I'm so glad you called. Happier; that we parted earlier and considered some of these things in our hearts and minds.

"Your honestly, tenacity, and concern are endearing my affection towards you, and my respect of you.

Had you not left my apartment, I'd likely be fast asleep with a smile on my face right now. And we may not have ever had this exact discussion. You are doing everything right to cause me to love you more in my heart, and in my head. This evening will be with me tomorrow, and each day after that, and yet somehow, I suspect we will continue to be amazed and exhilarated with the growth and depth of our love. It all seems so easy with you, Margo. I've been floundering around for years, now all of a sudden you appear. But it feels like you've always been right here. Sometimes I think I am dreaming my good fortune."

"Max, in the past I used to be the one in a relationship to suggest slowing down, taking our time. My reason and my intuition are telling me that you and I care coming together at the right time in our lives, under the right set of circumstances to make a solid, permanent, and happy life together. I am going to marry you when you are ready. So get yourself ready Max Bahle! Good night, my sweet!" She hung up the phone.

That afternoon at work I was outside refilling the pop machines. Not a customer was in the store. Margo came out and walked up behind me. She wrapped her arms around me. I felt her breath, then, she bit my ear. "Just in case you think you are dreaming," she coyly whispered.

A minivan slowly approached. The passenger window lowered. A family appeared lost. About that time Dad came out of the store, "Lovebirds, can you handle it from here? Think I'll drop by the Clubhouse then head home early."

"Goodnight, Will," Margo patted his shoulder.

"Anyone here know if this is the same Bahle as Max Bahle from Greenfield?" A male voice asked from the stopped van.

Stunned, I stopped what I was doing. Margo intently watched as I approached the van. Dad inched up behind me. "I'm Max Bahle. I used to live in Greenfield."

"I don't think your looks have changed that much," the driver said. "You taught school there, right?"

"One year," I replied.

"We were just driving around the area. I spoke at Augustana Lutheran in Elkton on Sunday. I'm a candidate there." He got out of the van, came around and said he wanted to introduce his family. He opened his wife's door, and the sliding door of the van. Two small boys bounded out. "I'm Dave Dunkel, by the way," he said as he shook my hand. "Doreen: my wife, our sons Dirk and Dustin."

"It's my pleasure to meet you all. This is Will, my dad. And this is Margo" –

"Lovebirds they are." Dad interrupted.

"Oh, how nice!" Doreen extended her hand. They each grabbed a boy and drew him close. They were very well mannered.

"I'm here because of you, Mr. Bahle. My parents took me to church when I was small. By the time I was in your class I didn't go with them. I was drunk a lot. I didn't care whether I passed or failed my classes until I had your class. Remember how you gave us all A's to start the year? Well, I accepted my A. I followed your instructions and kept my A. I worked hard. I recalled that it was for the under-achievers, us losers who you came to serve – and in some ways save us from lives of rejection."

"Somehow, I got into a junior college. Like most freshman, I wanted to take Psychology to see what was wrong with me, or my siblings or parents. I began journaling. I realized maybe it was the God culture of the community of my youth that was making me hostile, rebellious and confused. God was a boogey-man.

"The next semester I took a new testament survey course. It was taught like a history and literature course, but there were books on the reading list that exposed me to a liberal theology that I have spent the rest of my life since discovering. It works something like your class, Max. We're all born with an "A." That's God's grace gift to all humankind. We are sealed in that pact with baptism. The family, and the family of believers, the congregation that is, take a pledge, a vow to instruct and indoctrinate their young into their culture of belief.

"We can all choose to reject the comfort of grace. To break laws, injure ourselves or others and lose the heavenly peace we are given just for being there being part of God's creation. Just like your "A." It was ours to begin with just for showing up. I wanted to maintain that "A" so I did what was required for the prize. It wasn't just the "A" that was the result-ant prize. It was how I felt and thought about my-self. With God's grace I wanted to be respectful of the gift, to honor it. It caused me to behave more tolerantly of other's actions, ideas and attitudes. It caused me to become introspective and contempla-tive. I learned to regulate my selfish and destructive impulses and desires. Obviously, I wanted to share this notion of grace to assist others to choose more heavenly experiences than hellish ones for their own lives.

"I went back to church with my parents. The experience of being in your class made my earlier church indoctrination relevant. Suddenly, I felt loved by God. God's grace was available to me from the beginning. I just had to accept it; then my interest, desire, or faith would keep me acknowledging that grace gift, freely given to me, the underachiever, the loser.

"Do you see what I'm trying to say Mr. Bahle, Max?" Dave was looking at me.

"I think so. Anyway I'm glad my class helped you extrapolate all that if it has helped you become a whole person." I reached out to embrace Dave. But I did it for me. For almost two decades I had wondered, from time to time, whether I ever inspired a student or not. It is so much easier to let something from the past go, when it goes in peace. My teaching career of long ago would now slumber in peace for eternity. It had just been vindicated and validated by this caring man.

He looked at my dad, then Margo, "Even unwittingly, Max changed my life for the better."

"Well Dave," I began, "You did all of that for yourself. I had a small hand in it."

He replied, "I would gladly offer a small hand if I could add to your happiness.

"We had better be going." He loaded the boys into the van then closed his wife's door for her. "I'd love to be near Lake Ann;to pastor in Elkton would be amazing!" Dave spoke excitedly and hopeful.

I walked around to his side of the van. After he got in I leaned in the window, "Are you serious about lending me a small hand?" I asked.

"Yes, absolutely," he replied.

"Margo here, um, I want to marry her. If you get the church in Elkton"—

He interrupted,"Even if I don't get the church – yes! Yes!" He reached for a pad of paper to write down my phone number. A week later he called to tell me that the synod conference bishop would be installing him as senior pastor at Elkton's Augstana Lutheran Church during the Christmas season. He suggested we counsel sometime, but as we continued to talk on the phone he said, "Clearly beyond any doubt I believe God has worked to bring you and Margo together. I for one won't stand in the way of His plan!" He laughed.

Serious as a heartbeat I told him, "Pastor Dave, this completes a cycle now. Margo gives purpose and meaning to my living. And you will have a hand in it. I'll keep you informed," I told him.

As Dave and his family pulled away from the store, Margo stood beside me with her arm around me, her hand patting my side. "That was so wonderful!" she said happily.

"Son, you've waited too long to hear somebody tell you that you made a difference to their life. Finally it happened; good for you boy!" That said, Dad kissed the side of my head and turned to walk to his car, turning once to say, "Clubhouse, then home."

CHAPTER 5
PIE NIGHT

Thanksgiving was soon a blur of a memory. We filled special orders of every imaginable cut of meat. Deli items, pies and turkeys. Fresh dressed turkeys were our specialty. But we sold frozen as well. And we smoked them. At the holidays many of the summer residents would call in orders and drive from their permanent homes just to buy our products to serve at holidays.

The work was exhausting, but Thanksgiving kicks off a holiday season of excitement and exhilaration when folks seem a bit more cheery and purposeful.

Dad told Margo and I that things went smoothly; better than he could've dreamed of. Margo was astonished at the special orders, both the quantity and variety. As was customary around the holidays, Liz took the time off from her jobs to help with special orders at the store. Dad told Margo why Liz always worked in the back, and never at the counter, although she could clean up or run the cash register in a pinch.

One evening just before Thanksgiving we had been working late. So Dad said, "The store's buying dinner at the Clubhouse." We all went to Billie's.

Rich was there noisily screwing a thick sheet of plywood to a small stage riser in a dark corner of the bar. "What the hell's goin' on Rich?" Dad wanted to know.

"Join us!" Rich came over for a sandwich and a drink.

"Billie thought Hazel's picked up a few more pounds this year and wanted me to reinforce the stage for the upcoming pie night," he said.

"Whew! Pie Night!" Liz ballyhooed. "Oh my gosh – Margo! Do you know about pie night?"

"Speaking of night, I'll say night-night!" Dad said and left to go home.

"He's okay?" asked Rich.

"Yeah. He's okay. I mean he will have a rough day on Thanksgiving and Christmas. But we're going to change the routine. Now we've got Margo. We'll all be at her house on the holidays. That'll sure help." Liz explained.

"My pleasure to help however I can." Margo raised her glass and Liz 'clinked' hers.

"Now, pie night: Rich, you want to tell Margo about it?" Liz asked.

"Yeah. Everybody comes. It's always December 13, you know, about halfway between Thanksgiving and Christmas. Everybody brings a pie. Usually they are always, you know, pies, but sometimes somebody brings a pot pie or shepherd's pie. Those go fast. I've noticed that when there are less sweet pies, then there's less puking in the parking lot." Rich was serious. We all roared.

"Hazel always sings something just right and plays some kind of instrument," I continued.

"So she's more than the church organist?" Margo asked.

"Get a load of this" – Liz spoke almost frantic, "I'm accompanying her this year! I took piano lesions from her for five years, and do you know what she wants me to play? A Jew's harp!" she exploded with laughter. "That's all I can tell you. Be there or be square. Gotta go kids!" With that, my sister stepped out into the night, light-hearted and giddy from the silliness of the moment.

"Yeah, better clean up my mess and skeedaddle, too," Rich said.

"Sounds great," Margo seemed excited. I told her that Hazel also plays the piano, and folks sing Christmas carols. Usually a collection is taken for some family or person around town who has had a hardship.

"Max, you know a girl who dreams of being a

bride often has a Christmas list about this time of year," Margo bashfully admitted.

"List; you said list, not item," I noted. "Maybe you should show it to me sometime."

She reached for her purse, "Got it!" She laughed.

"Oh dear, I don't see yuletide corning ware anywhere on this list – guess I better return that!" I jested. The truth is; it wasn't a list, just a piece of paper with four pictures of rings. Simple band style rings.

"Just about anything like these would do. I thought it might help you," she said reservedly.

"I really, really appreciate this," I said. I folded it, put it in my pocket and said, "Margo, you make it so easy to be in love with you."

"How could you know what I want, if I don't tell you? I'm not setting you up for disaster. Never," she said, and leaning over, kissed me.

"Would you like to know what lil' Maxie wants for Christmas?" I played.

"I already know what lil' Maxie wants!" Margo said as she pinched my cheek. "And I've got it all under control."

The next morning at work things were going smoothly. I took off and headed to Elkton to a jeweler. It took longer than I supposed possible to select and order that engagement ring. I had a piece of string that I had earlier tied around Margo's finger. The jeweler didn't think that too reliable for sizing, but I assured him that any change needed would gladly be paid for.

Meanwhile, in my absence, Margo called Rich and instructed him to bring 'it' over to the store to show Will and Liz. She asked them if they would be around to see what she was thinking about giving to me for Christmas. They were excited. Rich arrived soon thereafter, with a shiny royal blue, restored 1958 Willy's pick-up truck.

"My heaven's I wish you were marrying me!" Dad exclaimed.

"Awesome!" Liz agreed.

"Do you think he's going to be okay with it, or will it offend him?" Margo genuinely wanted to know, "because, I've already bought it. Rich picked it up and checked it all out for me."

"Well, if he's got some problem with his Christmas present you let me know. I'll kick his ass," Dad seemed serious.

"I wouldn't be surprised that he has trouble accepting it at first. But you let us know honey, we'll talk to him," said Dad. And as he walked away laughing, he slapped Rich on the shoulder and said, "Got the world by the ass, that's what he's got. That's my boy! She's a looker, and she'd sell her curling iron to get him a pack of gum. That's just how it was for me, Rich," Dad said as he had his hand on Rich's shoulder.

"She was great. And you were a lucky man, Will," Rich replied.

"We'll make him give you his car then if it makes him feel better," Liz offered.

"Okay. Not a bad idea," Margo agreed.

Rich soon left. I eventually returned. The store was busy all afternoon right up to closing.

"Anybody besides me hungry for pizza?" Dad quizzed.

"Oh yeah!" Liz instantly spoke up.

"Okay by you, Margo? I asked. She nodded yes and I replied to Dad, "We're in."

"Dad's pizza is something to experience," Liz pointed out. "It's from scratch. Including the dough."

"Is that what's in the covered bowl on top of the refrigerator in back?" Margo wanted to know. "I thought I smelled something yeasty."

"That's it," Dad said. "Kinda learning to ignore some of the smells around here kiddo?" he asked Margo.

She smiled and nodded.

"The crust is fat and crispy on the outer edge. Then he puts about a teaspoon of pizza sauce on the entire thing. It has all this ground beef and ground ham and olives and onion and then about a foot of cheese. I guess it weighs about as much as a shoebox full of sand," Liz finished her description simply. "I really like it."

"I'm going to run home to clean up and change," began Margo, "then there's something I'm just dying to give Max."

"Oh, yeah. I'll just bet you've got something for Max," Liz was toying crudely, "But we don't want to know about it."

"And I want to show it to you, too," Margo spoke excitedly, and had either ignored Liz's comments entirely, or just hadn't caught on to the innuendo.

"Hopefully, we're thinking about different things," Liz continued to be ornery.

I went home, showered and changed clothes; and browsed through the mail. Then drove to Margo's to pick her up. As we drove to Dad's, she clutched a small package to her chest.

"You will never, not in a jillion years guess what this is my Max man!"

"You make surprises into celebrations, no, more like festivals," I pointed out.

"Max!" Margo exclaimed, and began to talk rapidly and excitedly as she ran through her mental list: "I'm a bit intoxicated with my life just now! I'm in love, I have a soon-to-be sister-in-law who has the time and kindness to be my friend, I have a soon-to-be father-in-law who speaks to me like a beloved child of his own, townspeople accept me and make me feel part of the community – interested in me – in us. I'm having a little trouble being down in the dumps these days," she finished jokingly.

We arrived at Dad's. The pizza was still in the oven. Liz clapped her hands and hopped up and down in mockery. "Oooh, let's see what Margo can't wait to give to Maxie."

Dad was at the sink scrubbing who knows what. I opened the package. "Looks like a video," Dad mentioned.

"Can we play it?" begged Margo. She had removed the label to make sure the whole thing was a surprise. Suddenly, a huge combine roared onto the picture screen.

"Oh, great! A farming video," Liz mocked.

"It's the great wheat harvest. It's a documentary," Margo stated happily as she watched me tune them all out and hang onto every word the narrator began to speak.

"Oh my gosh!" gasped Liz, "That's what Max always wanted to do when he was in college."

"What is it?" Dad came in at last.

Liz explained, "He may not be going on the harvest, but Margo got him a front row seat to it."

"Oh, here's a good part. I think this is a good part," Margo was pointing to the T.V. screen. A big truck pulled along side the combine, and the combine discharged the wheat into the truck as both operators continued to drive along.

"Sure is a lot of grain," Margo said.

"Sure is," Liz agreed.

The three of them walked back into the kitchen while I mentally transported briefly to the Great Plains.

Dad opened some beers for the girls and himself. As he sat down he said, "I think he spent ten years wanting to work the harvest. But never did. That was a creative and thoughtful gift, Margo."

"So are you going to be one of those hyphenated last named women?" Liz asked. "Or keep your name, or take Max's? What's up with all of that?"

"Fair question," Margo quickly replied, "I have thought about it a lot, too. Max said he didn't care, but preferred to not hyphenate his name. In the end, I sort of think he likes the simplicity of my choice."

"So what is it? Your choice," Dad was curious.

"If you think about it, I haven't chosen the name I have now. Mom and Dad made that choice. Now that I may choose for myself … are you ready?" Margo toyed with them, "I will be Margo Bahle."

Suddenly serious, Liz replied, "I never thought of it that way. That's pretty cool."

I joined them in the kitchen holding the tape. "Eighteen hour days," I said. "Those guys work 18 hour days. I don't know if I could've done that twenty years ago or not. But I wouldn't even want to now." I knelt down and touched Margo's face. "This is an amazingly thoughtful gift my dear. I can hardly wait until Christmas."

"Bet your ass!" Dad exclaimed and got up to serve his masterpiece.

We all ate like pizza pigs. Margo asked, "Why aren't we serving this in the deli?"

"It's a family thing," Dad quickly came back.

She persisted, "Well then I hope Max and Liz know how to do this, so we will always have this family thing."

We all sort of grunted. "Good point." And collectively considered that it would be a good thing if Liz or I or Margo, knew how to make Dad's pizza.

"So, do we each make a pie for pie night?" Margo asked.

"Sure do," Dad replied. "Pumpkin. That's all I ever take. It's the pie of the season. I couldn't think of making any other kind," he said.

"Besides, it's his favorite. He's kind of a pumpkin pie freak really," Liz pointed out, and patted his folded hands.

"What will you make, Liz?" Margo wanted to know.

"Probably like last year," Liz said. "You know those graham cracker crusts? I start with that. Then I get a can of whipped topping and squirt in until I fill the whole damn thing up!"

"Liz!" Dad was shocked.

"Ohhh, that was you!" I exclaimed. "I think I

tried to scoop up some of your pie last year – bad, bad girl!"

"Oh, come on!" Liz attempted to defend her actions. "There's like about – oh – eighty pies? Thirty percent don't get eaten, five percent end up trampled on the floor, a good ten percent get puked up in the parking lot. What's the difference?"

And no matter how old you get, now and then you are bound to hear what we heard from dad: "Now Liz, suppose everybody did that? Think what that would do to pie night."

"What about you, Max?" Margo asked. "Will we get together to make the ritualistic pie?"

"Oh, absolutely!" I declared. "I have a special fondness for that one dish coconut deal. It makes its own crust. Do you know about this? How can it do that? Just stir up this baking mix stuff and pour it into a pan all runny like pancake batter. Then viola! Pie! I can't believe it actually."

"Max, you need a bit more stimulation. You probably take notes watching the PBS special on toothbrush manufacturing," Liz started picking again. Then Margo played along.

"I think I saw that. Wow, it was really great!"

"Hey, good! This helps! I had narrowed down my choices for a wedding present. Now I've decided that the two of you would just be enthralled with a worm farm!" Liz was a champion smart-ass. I wondered if she would ever change, or find a man who was such an idiot that he couldn't tell when she insulted or ridiculed him.

"Goodnight! A wedding present!" Dad gasped. "I've got to get a wedding present for you kids."

"Oh, just go with my second choice, Dad," Liz went on, "The ant farm. They'll love to get it out and sit it on the table just to watch it by the hour, in case it changes color or shape or something."

"Your mom would've known exactly what to get." Dad spoke and lowered his head a bit. If fun was like a grand bonfire; then the small details, coming to the forefront of his mind were like great buckets of water thrown on the fire. We all wished we could take away Dad's recurring pain.

December 13th came during the week that year. So the night before, I took my baking mix and coconut and went to Margo's. An unrelenting bride-to-be she called her concoction "wedding pie." It had chopped nuts, whipped cream, cream cheese, pineapple, coconut, shredded chocolate and dried brightly colored cherries. Looked like a party on a plate. She had completed decorating her house for Christmas. Pine scented candles filled the kitchen with that unique holiday smell. Christmas music played softly. Everything was so perfect and wonderful that neither of us wanted me to leave. So I didn't.

The next day after work, we all rushed to Billie's. The place was wall to wall people. It didn't really have a starting point or an end, but somewhere early in the evening, generally after she had sampled a varietal plateful, Hazel would take the stage. This time it was with Liz, who had put her hair into pigtails, wore bib-overalls and tried to black out one of her eye teeth. Hazel stood there, leaned back, selected a note vocally and powerfully "sang" it as though she would shatter glass. Very quickly the party stilled.

"Welcome to pie night everyone. I'm accompanied by Miss Liz Bahle on the Jew's-harp, or mouth harp as it is commonly called, and in this case appropriately so. I loved Hazel giving Liz a dig like that. "As always we want to thank Billie for hosting our little tea party."

"A one: a two: a one, two, three, four!" Hazel spoke and stomped one foot loudly and took the bow to the fiddle partly lost under her chin, and then just tore that fiddle up before stopping between chanted verses:

I'll play for you on this here fiddle, I stomp my foot watch my big arms jiggle – 'cause I want pie!

I'll eat it hot, I'll eat it cold, I'll eat it with gravy, I've at it with mold – 'cause I want pie!

I eat it standing or sitting down. Once I had a slice in bed – he was from out of town- 'cause I want pie!

Fruit or cream filled are all fine as long as I can make it mine – 'cause I want pie!

She played the fiddle a bit more, then bowed and pointed to Liz and hollered, "My star pupil!"

People drank liquor, beer, wine, soft drinks, and of course, ate pie. No one left really feeling physically good; but having enjoyed the shared connection of a festive moment of collective craziness. That was the magical stuff that made belonging to a small community fun. At one point we sang Christmas carols. As the crowd thinned, music played on Billie's stereo. Margo and I danced.

Printed in the United States
751700001B